BLOOD ADEPT

A TEER & KARD STORY

BLOOD ADEPT

A TEER & KARD STORY

GLYNN STEWART

FAOLAN'S PEN
PUBLISHING
faolanspen.com

This edition published in 2023 by:

Faolan's Pen Publishing Inc.

22 King St. S, Suite 300

Waterloo, Ontario

N2J 1N8 Canada

ISBN: 978-1-989674-35-2 (print)

A record of this book is available from Library and Archives Canada.

Printed in the United States of America

1 2 3 4 5 6 7 8 9 10

First edition

First printing: May 2023

Illustration by Roman Chalyi

Faolan's Pen Publishing logo is a registered trademark of Faolan's Pen Publishing Inc.

Read more books from Glynn Stewart at faolanspen.com

1

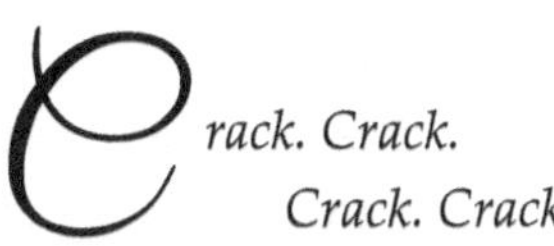

rack. Crack.
    Crack. Crack.
Crack. Crack.
Crack. Crack.

Eight shots rang out in eight heartbeats, each bullet punching through the dead center of the target and into the earth mound behind it.

Eight rounds clicked home into the short repeater over the next eight heartbeats, then Teer raised the gun to his shoulder and fired again.

Eight *cracks* rang out in six heartbeats this time, as he adjusted to the motion of the new gun and began to speed past normal human motions.

He had the cartridges for the cavalry weapon in a pouch open on the table in front of him. He wasn't even looking at the pouch as he drew the bullets out and loaded them into the repeater's magazine.

Six heartbeats, and then he opened fire again, trying to push the gun faster.

Teer had learned by now that few of the weapons built in the Unity of the Spehari could keep up with his speed. The short repeater was a solid lever-operated gun, taken from a group of bounty hunters who'd attacked him and his master, the half-blood El-Spehari Kard.

Unlike the silver-inlaid quickshooters lying next to the cartridge pouch or the blue-chromed hunter long rifle leaning against the table, the short repeater was a *good* gun but not one of the best in the Eastern Territories. The quickshooters had belonged to the *leader* of the bounty hunters who'd attacked them, and the hunter had been a gift from his stepfather.

Those three weapons were each, in their own way, masterpieces of the gunsmith's art. The short repeater, on the other hand, was a standard weapon issued to the cavalry forces of the Unity. Rarely seen outside the hands of cavalry troopers, it held the stigma of being the main weapon of the Sunset Rebellion of Teer's childhood.

The Rebellion where his father had died.

"Teer is learning," his instructor's voice said cheerfully. "Tyrus saw you slow when the mechanism struggled. Good."

Teer was a gawky dark-skinned youth of the Merik, the "first among slaves" of the Spehari Unity. His people had been the first the Spehari had conquered and had formed the bulk of the armies that had broken most known lands to Spehari will over the following centuries.

Tyrus, on the other hand, was a squat and muscular man with dark blue skin. Scars marked the Kotan shaman's arms and face, including where he'd lost an eye. *His* people, unlike Teer's, were still mostly free of the Unity.

Which, of course, the Unity did *not* like. Teer and Kard were there because they'd escorted a refugee from Unity law to join the Kotan tribe Tyrus led—and so that Tyrus could teach Teer how to use his own gifts.

"Slow is learning," Tyrus continued, stepping up next to Teer and tapping for him to put the repeater down. "Learning is skill. Skill is speed. But guns… Guns are not designed for Kota who ride Cauldron. And if guns were ever made for Merik like Teer, they are long lost."

"Destroyed," Teer guessed.

"Likely. If Kard knows nothing of talents like Teer's…" Tyrus shrugged. "Not all Kota shamans can ride the Cauldron, Teer. Not all who ride Cauldron ride fast enough to challenge guns. Some ride fast enough that even bows cannot keep up."

"The Cauldron?"

"Cauldron is why Tyrus can teach Teer," the shaman told him. "Tyrus has prepared it. But for now, Teer must learn at speed of child. Some of Teer's arms can hold much of Teer's speed. But no mechanism of factory make will hold a Notable Shaman riding the Cauldron…and Kard believes Teer can match that."

Tyrus laid a leather-wrapped package Teer hadn't noticed on the table.

"Kard found this after Tyrus asked," Tyrus told him. "Tyrus did not ask where. Tyrus knows every blade in Tyrus's tribe. This is not one of them."

Teer slowly unwrapped the blade and shivered as he looked down at it. He'd been a ranch hand before his fateful meeting with Kard. He was familiar with both the big working knives of cattlehands and the equally large cleavers of butchers and slaughterhouses.

He had no familiarity with bladed *weapons*, but he recognized the brutal efficiency of the one he was looking at. It was longer than any knife he'd ever seen, easily half again the length of his arm, with a curve to the blade that made its use for slashing obvious even to him.

"Tyrus knows the pattern," the shaman observed. "Unity cavalry saber. But this blade…"

Something in Tyrus's voice told Teer that the Kota had hoped to never see a sword like this again. Even as Teer's gaze traced the lines of the blade—the *pattern*, as Tyrus named it—he could feel there was something subtly off about the sword.

For one thing, he'd never seen steel that dark. A faint wavelike pattern was visible in the midafternoon light, but even *that* was a burgundy red that reminded him of the setting sun.

"What is it, Tyrus?" Teer asked.

"Kott."

Teer shivered. He hadn't met any of the Kott, but the lizardlike people who'd fought alongside the Prince in Sunset in his rebellions were known across the Unity. Unity armies had chased the Kott back into their swamps after the rebellions, but the war since had been unending and bloody.

"So, Kard had this just…in his saddlebags?" Teer asked.

"Ask Kard," Tyrus said sharply. "Tyrus is here to teach Teer to use a blade. We start at child pace. Tyrus must know Teer will not cut self."

The young cattlehand felt like he almost *should* be offended by that, except that something in how Tyrus said it made it very matter-of-fact. And left Teer suspecting that at least one youth Tyrus had trained had done *exactly* that.

———

TEER WAS USED TO GUNS. He didn't miss with guns except for the very first shot he took with a given firearm.

He was *not* used to swords, and the first candlemark of training with Tyrus was a mix of humiliating and exhausting. The first hints of twilight were starting to appear in the sky when the shaman finally let him rest.

"Not bad," Tyrus concluded. "Need work, but Teer never held a sword before. So, not bad."

"Thanks," Teer said. An attractive, petite young woman in a freshly sewn dress appeared at the edge of the training ground with a tray of drinks. Gesturing the two of them over to her, she put the tray on the table he'd rested his gear on.

Lora then proceeded to very thoroughly kiss Teer, a pleasant endeavor that left the tips of his ears flushing pink. She was the refugee he and Kard had brought to the Kota, and he wasn't entirely sure where their relationship was going—or even *could* go, given that she couldn't return to the Unity without facing the charges and twisted court they'd rescued her from.

He couldn't stay with the Kota and she couldn't leave. Even Teer wasn't foolish enough to miss what that meant, but for the moment, he was enjoying her company and attention.

"Kard went out with one of the patrols," she told Tyrus. "He said that Shaman Nia hasn't returned yet and it's making him anxious."

Teer took a sip of the cooled tea Lora had brought—a desperately needed beverage after the day of intensive training. They'd been in the Kota settlement for three days now, and they'd met Shaman Nia on their way in.

"She was huntin' the callipsus, right?" he asked. "That's not good."

"But Teer killed the callipsus," Lora said, a spark of fear tensing her shoulders.

Teer shivered at the memory. The callipsus Nia had been hunting was a large lizard-like creature—and not in the way of the Kott, who apparently looked much like Merik or Spehari for all that they had scales and cooler blood. A callipsus looked like the watch-lizards he was familiar with from the plains, four-legged creatures that would sun themselves on rocks and watch humans and cattle pass.

Except that a watch-lizard was a foot long, excluding its tail, and ran on all four legs. A callipsus was closer to *twelve* feet long and stood on its hind legs, freeing its forearms for limited manipulation and an ugly claw on its hind legs for kicking.

They also commanded powerful magic of their own and fed, when they could, on sentient beings.

"Teer killed a *young* callipsus," Tyrus said grimly. "Too young to be long away from its parent. No, Nia's prey still haunts these hills. A five-day hunt for a callipsus is not strange."

"But it worries Kard," Teer said.

"And perhaps Tyrus, but Tyrus cannot say such," the shaman replied. "Lora makes excellent cool tea, Tyrus must observe. But Tyrus has worked poor Teer to the edge of Teer's pride, if not Teer's endurance.

"Come, let us eat." The old shaman gestured toward the round structure at the center of the settlement, his current home. "Whatever comes, we must all be ready for it."

2

After several days among the Kota, Teer was clear on one thing: he had *no* idea how the Kota organized themselves. Tyrus was a "Notable Shaman" and everyone seemed to look to him for guidance —but he was quite clearly not in charge, though his house was at the center of the settlement.

The entire town was built of near-identical structures. All of them were round, straight-walled buildings with red-thatched roofs. The red in the thatch came from the massive natural hedge that surrounded them, the redgrave trees that covered the entire summit of the hill and concealed the Kota from prying eyes.

Kotan magic, he'd been told, shaped the redgrave to their needs. Paths were woven through the grove, not cut, and most of the smaller pieces of wood in the town were clearly deadfall from the redgrave trees.

He wasn't sure where the tall straight wooden pillars that held up the structures came from, but they clearly weren't from the redgraves. The sacred trees didn't grow tall enough for the timbers in the permanent structures.

Many of the tribe's people lived in tents, in a large area set aside for them inside the clearing. Tyrus wasn't the only person living in the roundhouses, Teer had seen, but even the occupied buildings served as common space.

Lora had taken over cooking at Tyrus's roundhouse—which served both as home to the tribe's shamans and as the main school—the day after she'd arrived. Teer wasn't sure how that had happened, but he *did* know that the food at the shaman's table had improved noticeably once she had taken over!

By the time she led Teer and Tyrus back into the roundhouse, several others were already seated around the table. Tyrus gestured the two young Merik to join the others and vanished into his own room.

"Young Teer, be welcome," the stranger at the table told him.

Teer knew the two shamans at the table: Reeah and Tala. The town's machine-worker, Ryle, was responsible for their mix of stolen and purchased Unity machine tools—and a few mechanisms of her own making.

The stranger shared the same build as Tyrus, a massive-shouldered man with blue skin only a shade paler than Lora's near–midnight black. He wore a corset and trousers, like most of the Kota, and lacked the colored scarves of the shamans.

"Sir," Teer greeted the man, taking the seat Lora guided him to— next to hers.

"I am Notable Leader Sho," the stranger told him with a smile. "As Tyrus leads the tribe's minds and hearts, Sho guards the paths and borders. Tyrus commands power. Sho…merely leads."

"Sho returns from scoutin' the farmlands west o' here," Reeah explained.

"Sho heard words of concern," Sho noted. "And Sho finds… Ach."

He picked up a wooden flagon and took a large swallow of something.

"When Tyrus joins us, Sho will speak of that. For now. Young Teer, young Lora, you are new guests in the Kota's homes. Speak freely; have Teer and Lora been made welcome?"

"Lora has asked for sanctuary and Tyrus granted," Lora murmured, clearly trying to emulate the Kota's odd speech patterns. "Not a guest, I hope."

"Your people are kind and welcomin'," Teer said. "Tyrus has

offered words and wisdom I don't think anyone else could. I wait on Kard, of course, but we are here for a reason."

"Teer is Kard's Bondservant, yes," Sho observed. "Do not fear, Lora; Lora is welcome here. Lora will be one of us. In time." He shrugged. "Forgive this old warrior Sho's misspeak.

"Lora is new to Kota, and only time will make Lora Kota. But the Kota are Lora's home, as long as Lora desires."

"The Unity would hang me over a wardstone."

Lora's flat words said everything, Teer knew. The wardstones, the centerpieces of Unity wardtowns, served as magical defenses, communication tools and weather mitigators for the towns. But they required restoring on a regular basis, either through the power of one of the Spehari themselves...or the sacrifice of a living person.

"Lora will find none here who love the Unity." Sho stared off into the distance. "Like Tyrus, Sho rode with Sunset. Sho never..."

"Sho realized what Tyrus did not," said Tyrus, exiting his room and crossing to the head of his table. "The Prince in Sunset was a good man. But he was El-Spehari and he did not know how to be less than a demigod.

"The Prince's world would have been softer on those in the Unity... but Sho knew then that the Unity would still expand. Tyrus was not so wise."

Tyrus had changed out of the heavy buff jacket he'd worn for training, swapping to a plain blue kilt that left his chest bare and a long purple scarf woven through his hair and over his eye.

"Rivers flow, moons rise." Sho shook his head and reached over to squeeze Tyrus's hand. "To fight the King in Winter was a worthy cause."

"Sho returns later than Tyrus hoped," Tyrus observed as Reeah slid the Notable Shaman a plate of food. "But Sho now meets Lora's cookin'. Tyrus suggests appreciation."

The Kotan warrior chuckled.

"So, that's why the food is good," he said. "Sho cooks when here, but Tyrus tries to feed Tyrus otherwise." Sho paused, letting his words hang in the air as he smiled at what Teer presumed was his lover.

"Tyrus is a very bad cook."

The shaman sighed melodramatically, then shrugged.

"Tyrus must agree. But Tyrus must set example. Sometimes, that means Tyrus cook. Sometimes, that means Tyrus takes new child under wing. Both duties, in own way."

Teer squeezed Lora's hand. He suspected she was overwhelmed by how much her life had changed—but he also knew where the scars under her dress were. The ones that marked where a Merik businessman pet of the Spehari had tried to use a forbidden magic to steal turnings from her life.

The problem was that one of the Marked, the chosen servants of the Spehari, were not *quite* above the law. What had been done to Lora was against Unity law—so, given that she'd beaten her attacker to the edge of death in self-defense, the man had made *her* the criminal.

And his influence meant she'd never get a fair court. She would be killed to protect the Marked's secrets.

So, there she was. Being the "new child" Tyrus was taking under his wing.

Teer had sympathy for her situation, beyond their physical involvement. He had run afoul of the Unity's laws as well. The price in his case had been to become magically and legally bound to an El-Spehari.

The *problem* was that while Kard could exercise the authority of his father's race so long as no one asked questions, the El-Spehari had been central to the Sunset Rebellion. Few of them remained, and all were supposed to be bound by magic to the King in Winter.

Kard wasn't. There were people, the Inquisitors, whose entire job was to find El-Spehari like Kard—and Teer had now bound his life and fate to the other man.

Sighing, he finished his own tea and plate, leaning forward on the table.

"Sho is late," Tyrus finally repeated. "Sho dodge the question, but Tyrus is too old to be fooled. Especially as Tyrus knows Sho very well."

Sho spread his hands.

"Tyrus does," he agreed. "Sho presumes all here are trusted?"

"All are tribe but Teer," the shaman replied. "And Teer is Bonded to Kard, who is *more* than tribe to Tyrus and Sho."

"Aye," Sho rumbled, eyeing Tyrus for a few long heartbeats. "Sho not know the Bond well, but Sho knows Kard. If Tyrus trusts Teer, is enough."

"Stop dancing and speak," Tyrus commanded.

Sho chuckled and nodded.

"Sho led a dozen scouts to survey the farms to the west," he told the table. "Unity draws farther east each turning of the seasons, but not all Unity settlers are lost. Kota can trade with some. Kota can warn others."

"Kota must destroy few…but *few* is not *none*," Tyrus warned.

"Kota try to avoid that," Sho said. "It draws attention, and Unity attention comes with soldiers and guns. Sho leads the warriors of this tribe. They are brave Kota. But Kota warriors cannot stand against Unity armies when ten soldiers march against each Kota.

"And they have cannons."

Teer had rarely seen more than a couple dozen Unity soldiers at once and had only seen Unity cannons in forts. Still, he could envisage the kind of force Sho spoke of and could tell that the unnamed town around them had no real defense against it.

"So, Sho scout the farms," Sho concluded. "Find friends, learn foes, recognize who is…neither. In some ways, all are foes, but…Kota cannot win that war. No tribe has stood against Unity. Sho not believe any ever could, not since Merik knelt."

There was no judgment in Sho's words, but Teer still shivered to hear them. It was one thing to be a child of the Merik and recognize their first-after-the-gods status. It was another to hear someone blandly state that *your people* had been the only ones who could have stopped the enslavement of a continent.

"Sho found something new among the settlers?" Tyrus asked.

"Sho found *nothing* where there should have been settlers," the scout leader said flatly. "Empty farms. Loose herds. Broken buildings. Sho knows signs, found tracks. A callipsus has been feeding along the Unity's frontier."

"A breeding pair," the shaman replied. "They have consumed enough innocents to spawn. A juvenile was found, killed. The breeding pair not yet. Nia hunts them."

Sho shook his head.

"Then worse than Tyrus fears," he said.

Teer, who had a cursed good idea of what Tyrus feared, sat up straighter at Sho's words.

"Time," Sho continued. "Time is what Tyrus forgets. A juvenile… How large?"

"Teer?" Tyrus turned to the young Merik.

"Taller than a man," Teer said. "Six, seven feet. Enough magic to fool Kard."

He'd been able to see through its illusions—but even *Kard's* illusions had no hold on Teer's vision. It had been the first sign to the El-Spehari that something was different about Teer.

Well, that and the fact that Teer had thought Kard was a full-blooded Spehari and tried to *shoot* him.

"Callipsuses do not age like Kota," Sho murmured. "Nor like Merik, or Spehari. Closer to Kott, but…a callipsus the height of a man has seen ten, twelve turnings. It was not born of the feedings among the farms at the feet of the Venedors."

The Venedors were the hills the redgraves grew over. The ones that concealed the Kota tribe's town.

"None of that horror was more than a season past," the scout warned. "They are spawning *again*."

Tyrus sighed and gestured roughly.

"Tyrus did not think of the timing of a juvenile," he admitted. "Nor, Tyrus fears, did Kard. If they have an *egg*…we are not ready to face this foe."

"We will *never* be ready to face a brooding callipsus pair," Sho declared. "One old enough to have spawned already? Hundreds have died to feed this monster. Our few dozens of scouts and handful of real war guns cannot fight a mated pair.

"But the Kota need not fight them," he said with a sigh. "For the Unity is not blind to the monster on their border. Sho sent Leeock into the town at Shellsvan. Shellsvan is not yet a wardtown, but they are close.

"Word has been sent to the west and word has returned east. The Unity has heard the call. They are sending soldiers."

"No, Sho," Tyrus said softly. "If the Unity have heard the call and believe there is a callipsus, they are not sending mere soldiers. The Unity will send a *Spehari*. And that means the Kota must leave before the Kota planned."

"That is not Tyrus's decision," Sho replied. "Nor Sho's."

"Sho and Tyrus must summon council."

"Agreed."

Teer had no idea what that meant, but he wasn't sure he liked the idea of the Kota leaving. He didn't know where they would go, but he *did* know that Lora would go with them.

He'd thought they would have more time. From the way she was clutching his hand under the table, so had she.

But even as he was about to ask what "summon council" meant, he heard something. He had learned that he had sharper senses than anyone else in the room. A Kota shaman like Tyrus had sharper-than-ordinary senses, but it required a specific potion for them to match Teer's regular hearing.

"Tyrus...there is trouble at the edge of town," Teer said. "I hear shoutin'."

He swallowed a hard stone in his stomach, his sense of Kard's presence twinging.

"Kard is here," he continued. "And I hear Nia's name."

3

eer's connection with Kard told him where the El-Spehari was. It also told him that the El-Spehari was uninjured, but that was all it really gave him. He couldn't assess his master and friend's state of mind or anything like that until he was much closer.

Still, he was unsurprised as he and the rest of the dinner group reached the edge of the town to find Kard and a handful of Kota warriors pulling a series of improvised sleds.

The El-Spehari was giving orders and people were following them. That, in Teer's experience so far, seemed to be the basis of almost all Kotan hierarchy and authority—if you knew what you were doing, the Kota would listen.

"Tyrus, thank the Pillars," Kard declared as Teer and the shaman approached. "I stabilized everyone I could, but just holding this many people together is taking everything I've got."

"What happened?" Tyrus demanded.

"Nia found callipsus, we thought," one of the standing scouts told the shaman. "Nia had a plan. Soth and others executed, lured callipsus into crossfire."

The scout—Soth?—shivered.

"It was smaller than Soth expected," she admitted. "Already

wounded, Nia realized. Scouts killed it, but there were…more. Soth was checking on the perimeter when they arrived. At least two… maybe more."

"Iron Pillars," Kard cursed. "We hadn't had time to catch up while we were making sure nobody died," he told Tyrus. "I found Soth with half a dozen not-quite-dead scouts and Nia, doing everything she could to keep the others alive."

"Nia… The others… They were the ones I could drag away while the callipsuses were…"

"Feeding," Tyrus finished for the scout. "Rest, child," he told Soth. "Soth could not have saved the dead. Soth saved the living. More could not have been asked."

The scout slumped, leaning on one of the Kota who'd gone out with Kard.

Tyrus, meanwhile, was gesturing the two younger shamans who'd shared the dinner table with them to take on the least-wounded of the hunting party as he knelt by Nia herself.

"Lora," he called softly. "Can Lora run back to the roundhouse for Tyrus? Blue-stained leather bag is by Tyrus's room. Bring quickly."

"Of course!"

Teer's girlfriend shot off like a spooked rabbit.

Teer stood there feeling useless. *He* had no healing magic—just the emergency training any cattlehand riding a ranch had. Soth had already done everything Teer knew how to do!

"Teer and Sho will keep area clear; help them get to shelter," Sho told him.

Grateful for the instruction, Teer immediately joined the Kota scout leader. He had neither magic nor mundane healing skills that could save lives today. But he could definitely *help* those who did!

———

THE SUN HAD SET into darkness and firstmoon was up by the time the wounded had been stabilized. Teer and Sho stood guard outside the roundhouse that served as a clinic for the Kotan town—not that a guard was really needed except for people's nerves.

Firstmoon's scant glow was being joined by the first spots of secondmoon light when Tyrus emerged from the roundhouse with Kard in tow.

"They will all live," Tyrus declared. "Thanks to Kard and Soth."

"Soth will not forgive Soth soon," Sho judged. "Sho has seen it before."

"We all have," Kard said. "Teer, are you all right?"

"I just trained today," Teer murmured. "I'm glad you found 'em."

"I should have gone out yesterday," the El-Spehari said grimly. "Wouldn't have changed anything, but Soth got two of them away that died before I found them."

"Strange that the callipsuses let Soth sneak their prey away," Sho said.

"They're brooding," Kard said flatly. "And grieving. They are not animals, remember that. And Nia and her warriors killed their child. The pair grieves and guards their remaining egg. If there are more than a pair, though…"

"They have spawned before," Tyrus concluded. "Multiple adults, a juvenile and a new egg. How many innocents have died to feed this monstrous family?"

"Too many." The El-Spehari shook his head. "They have no choice, I suppose, but I will not forgive the kind of slaughter the callipsuses carry out. Even the Unity hunts them."

"And so the Unity does," Sho warned. "These callipsuses are hunted. A company of cavalry have been promised to the local town, but Tyrus warns that—"

"They will send Spehari." Kard's voice was colder than Teer had ever heard. "This will require a very careful game."

"Not for the Kota, Tyrus fears," the shaman said. "We must move. This part of the Venedors is no longer safe for us—with callipsuses hunting the hills and the Unity marching their army to the plains, the Kota cannot remain."

"Again, Tyrus, that is not Tyrus's decision," Sho pointed out. "Summon council. The tribe must move, Sho agrees, but it is the council's decision."

"Agreed. We will summon council," Tyrus conceded. "Tyrus does not know what Kard will do, but the Kota must speak as one."

"There is only one thing I can do," Kard replied. "Callipsuses hunt the innocent and guilty alike. I must return the favor."

"Where you go, I go," Teer pointed out, stepping over to stand by his master.

"I know. That makes it a bit harder, but I swore an oath, long ago."

"Three callipsuses, Lord Colonel," Sho pointed out. "Sho has seen Kard's power, but that is a great threat."

"That's why we will need to walk a careful path," Kard replied. "Because Teer and I cannot defeat three callipsuses on our own, no. We need the Unity. They will send a Magistrate, soldiers and cannons. We need them all.

"If we are careful, we can work with them without them ever realizing what I am—or what Teer is."

Teer chuckled.

"If they realize what I am, do you think they'll tell me?" he asked. Teer only really knew that he wasn't an ordinary Merik.

"I do not imagine there are many Spehari who *would* know what you are," Kard said grimly. "But given that there are no other Merik like you anymore, I only see one reason for that rarity."

Teer's chuckle turned to a wince. He'd drawn the same conclusion already—it was part of why they'd come to Tyrus to teach Teer how to use his full speed and strength. Teer was faster and stronger than *Kard*, even when the El-Spehari used magic to augment his physical abilities.

Tyrus could "ride the Cauldron," as the shaman had described using the augmenting potion he'd brewed, to match Teer's abilities for a short time. A full-blooded Spehari could probably match Teer as well.

Plus, for all of his strength, speed and senses, Teer had no illusions who would win in a remotely fair fight between him and Kard. The El-Spehari was older, wiser and far better trained with his more extensive powers.

"We will attend council," Kard told the two Kota leaders. "But then I think Teer and I will need to pack and go our own way."

4

"Summoning council," it turned out, was a relatively simple matter of telling everyone in earshot that Tyrus and Sho were doing so. Those people went out looking for other members of the tribe, who told other members of the tribe, who told others, and so on and so forth.

By the time firstmoon and secondmoon were full in the sky, the entire population of the redgrave-enshrouded town had gathered in the open area in front of Tyrus's roundhouse.

For his own part, Teer was dressed for the hunt. He and Kard were officially Unity bounty hunters, and both of them had heavy gray coats with steel plates woven through them. Even a callipsus's claws would struggle against the armored greatcoats.

And while the Venedors were northerly and warm, night brought a sharp chill with it that made Teer glad for the heavy garment. Few of the Kota seemed bothered, most still wearing their apparently traditional trousers and corset-style tops.

He hadn't realized there were quite so many people in the town. Teer had known there were a few hundred at least, but his focus on his own affairs and the callipsus threat had kept him from really realizing the size of the tribe.

There were easily a thousand Kota gathered in the open spaces of the settlement now. Lamps he hadn't seen before had been raised up on poles, scattering an unusually bright light across the meeting.

The lamps weren't anything Teer was familiar with. He was used to gas or refined animal fat lanterns—or the redcrystal magical lights made by the Spehari. In his time among the Kota, he'd only seen torches or candles before.

This light was new, but it allowed the crowd to see clearly as Tyrus, Sho, and an elderly Merik woman Teer hadn't met yet walked out of the roundhouse to look over their people.

"Kota are in council," Tyrus announced formally. "Let those who guide speak, friends, but then all may speak their piece."

There was a level of silence in the crowd that Teer found surprising. The Kota he had known—all but one of whom were in this council— were independent, fractious and talkative people.

Yet they were perfectly silent now. He stood by Kard's side, waiting to hear how much Sho and Tyrus shared with their people. He was under no illusion that the scout and the shaman actually *ruled* the tribe, but they certainly seemed to *lead* it.

"Kota all know that Sho scouts the Unity farms," Sho told them. "Last trip ran long because Sho found worries. Empty farms. Missing settlers. Not perhaps a bad thing for Kota, but the cause is always a fear.

"Callipsuses hunt around the Venedors. Not just one—as Kota believed before—but a mated pair. Innocents have died, and the Unity answers."

"The Unity rarely fixes a problem with a feather where a cannon can be used," Tyrus warned. "And the callipsuses are not a problem easily fixed. They will send Spehari and armies."

"Those armies are a threat to the Kota," Sho concluded. "So are the callipsuses. Between the beasts and the Unity, the Venedors are no longer safe for us. Sho advise that we flee to the northeastern home."

"Tyrus is less specific," the shaman observed. "But yes, Tyrus feels we must leave."

"Ada shares their fears," the old Merik woman said. "Ada has the seen the way the Unity handles a crisis. A Unity army near us will learn of us and will determine that we must be brought into Unity. Ada concurs with the Notable Shaman and the Notable Leader."

Once the three people in front of the gathering finished speaking, the silence faded into a chaos closer to what Teer had expected. *He* couldn't follow the questions and comments, but it was clear that the three at the front were keeping track.

Interestingly, he realized that Tyrus, Sho and Ada weren't *answering* the questions. Other members of the tribe were. The discussion ebbed and flowed across the crowd in a way he recognized he had neither the experience nor the training to follow.

Likely, not all of the Kota were fully following the discussion. But every question was getting answered, and the three speakers waited for the hubbub to slow to a dull roar.

"Ada judges the tribe ready to take a call," the dark-skinned woman observed. "All in favor of moving to the northeastern home?"

Hands were raised across the crowd. Teer had once learned to count cattle on the run, so counting the hands and votes took him moments. It seemed a clear majority to him, but Ada raised her voice again.

"All in favor of remaining here?"

Some hands went up, but it was clear that the decision was made.

"Well, it's not Ada's job to tell the tribe what to do," Ada declared. "But the vote is for the northeastern home. Council is decided and council is released. Kota all have packing to do."

The crowd started to disperse as smoothly and calmly as it had gathered. Teer had seen similarly calm meetings in his life—but they'd been "family meetings" of everyone on his stepfather's ranch. There'd only been twenty or so people in those gatherings.

Yet the Kota had managed a similarly organized and complete discussion with over a thousand in less than a candlemark.

He was impressed. It helped that he even agreed with the decision —though as he spotted Lora weaving her way through the crowd toward him, he knew it was going to cause him pain.

———

LORA PULLED Teer away from the crowd, back into Tyrus's roundhouse. Even there, the junior shamans were starting to go through things and make lists, though Teer suspected that list-making would be all that happened that evening.

Packing up the town would be at least a full-day process and more likely two. Even that would be impressive to Teer, but he figured the Kota knew the task before them. *He* didn't, but they'd clearly done this before.

"I figured we'd 'ave more time," Lora finally told him, taking a seat out of the way and studying Teer.

Even without her being seated, Teer was taller and broader than she was. Right now, he was vividly aware of her limited size. He *knew* her apparent frailty was an illusion—she'd killed a man to save her own life once, and another to save *his* life.

"So did I," he admitted to her. "But we…we knew."

"You could come with," she said. "I don't know everything, but I know you still training. Tyrus is teaching you and he's only 'ad a few days."

"I can't." He shook his head and sighed. "I go where Kard goes, Lora. That choice is bound to my blood now. I cannot break it."

If he was being honest, Teer wasn't even entirely sure *Kard* could break it—and he had suspicions about the consequences for him if Kard died. Plus…

"We can't let a *pack* of callipsuses roam free," he said. "Sho says they'd killed dozens at least. Kard warned they'll kill more. We have to stop 'em."

"Why?" At his sharp look, Lora shook her head defensively. "I know they need stoppin'. But why does it need to be you and Kard? The Unity is sending an army."

"'Cause we're here and we can help," Teer replied. "Kard has power. I have…*something*. We have guns and magic and we know what we're fightin'. The Unity doesn't know what they're comin' for.

"I hate all that the Unity stands for, but the soldiers who'll ride out 'gainst those beasts? They'll *die*, Lora, 'cause the Unity thinks there's only one.'Gainst three?"

He shook his head.

"I don't know what they're bringin', but I don't think they're ready for the enemy they're gonna face."

Lora sighed and reached out a hand to him. He took it and squeezed her fingers, his skin pale only in comparison to hers.

"So, that's it, then?" she murmured. "You and Kard ride off to save the day and I never see you again?"

"Can't say never," Teer said. "We may follow the Kota to finish my training. I don't know yet. But first, we have to deal with the callipsuses. We can't be the protectors and hunters we're supposed to be if we walk away from this kind of threat."

5

Star was, in Teer's experienced opinion, an extremely good horse. She was a well-behaved dark brown mare who'd been raised and trained to be a cattle horse. She'd taken to the life of a bounty hunter's main mount with surprising calm and grace, carrying Teer into and out of trouble.

He had just finished brushing her when he heard and felt Kard walk up behind him.

"Teer. You ready?"

"Aye. What's the plan?" Teer asked. He'd prepared supplies—food, cartridges, clothes, the usual collection for a long-distance ride—but he didn't know exactly what Kard was thinking.

"I am…not entirely certain," the El-Spehari admitted. "I think our best option is to ride to Shellsvan and see what the locals are saying. The callipsuses will have cleared their tracks from the fight with Nia and her warriors.

"As I keep trying to remind everyone, they're *not animals*."

Teer shivered at Kard's fierceness on the last words.

"I'm not sure I follow what you mean, Kard," he said.

"It's easy to think about a callipsus as a wolf or a wolfen," Kard told him. "A dangerous animal, writ large and with strange abilities.

But they're not. They are *people*, just as smart as you or I, and with their own goals.

"The problem is that, like most Merik and Kota and Kott and…" Kard left the long list unfinished as he sighed. "Like most people, they want to have children. And for a callipsus to spawn, both of the mated pair must consume at least a dozen thinking brains.

"So, a species as long-lived and powerful as the callipsus is a threat the Unity—indeed, *any* group of people—cannot tolerate existing. There can be no negotiation, no peace, between predator and prey.

"We will protect our weak and vulnerable, and they will attempt to feed on them." Kard stared grimly off into the wall of redgraves around the town. "So, it is war between our species. But we have to remember that it is *war*, against an enemy just as smart, just as magically powerful and notably physically superior. Treating them as animals is a way to get a lot of people killed."

"So, what do we do?" Teer asked.

"We fight." Kard shrugged. "Are you ready to ride?"

"Yeah." Teer considered the situation with Lora, then sighed. "Yeah. Everything here is sorted. I have my guns; I've packed saddlebags. I'm ready."

"Lora?" the El-Spehari asked, following Teer's thoughts.

"We talked after the council last night. It's not what either of us was hopin' for, but…we knew it would be short, no matter what."

"All right. Get Star loaded up. I'm going to go find—"

"Tyrus?" Tyrus interjected with a chuckle. "Tyrus is here, Lord Colonel."

Kard sighed.

"Turnings upon turnings," he told the Kota. "The flow of time and sun and water have passed, and *yet* you still call me by that title."

"Kard earned Kard's title in blood and fire," Tyrus replied. "To the Kota, titles never die."

He'd said the same thing, word for word, when Teer had first met him. It felt like an argument that had been ongoing for a long, *long* time. Teer knew, now, that Kard had once been Lord Colonel Karn of House Morais, commander of one of the Sunset Brigades and a right-hand man of the Prince in Sunset.

He wasn't certain he fully understood what all of that *meant* beyond that his boss had been a key member of the rebellion that had killed his father. He *definitely* hadn't known all of the details when he'd sworn his life to Kard's service—but the alternative had been death.

Service had been the only way out Kard had found for him.

"Kard and Teer ride to the hunt," Tyrus observed after a few moments of silence. "But as Teer learned, callipsuses do not fear bullets."

"The one I shot survived, but Nia finished it off," Teer said. "That's what we're guessing, yes?"

He'd shot the creature through the top of its mouth. Teer did not, as a rule, miss—which made the callipsus's survival surprising.

"Yes," the shaman confirmed. "Callipsus skin is tough, Teer, even on the inside. Even if pierced, the bullet loses power. And callipsus heals."

Tyrus shook his head grimly and produced a pair of pouches woven from redgrave leaves.

"Tyrus not fight for Unity serfs," he said bluntly. "Tyrus look to and guard Kota tribe Tyrus serves. But Tyrus not stand wholly aside, either. Tyrus send gifts with Tyrus's friends, gifts to save innocents.

"Even if Unity serfs not under Tyrus's protection, innocents deserve guardians."

Kard took the two pouches and handed one to Teer. Something in the care the El-Spehari took with the packages told Teer that his boss knew what Tyrus was giving them.

"Bullets not lend themselves to Kota magic," Tyrus observed. "But can be...convinced, given effort. Two dozen cartridges in each pouch. Fit repeaters. Maybe Teer's hunter. Not quickshooters."

Teer nodded slowly as he opened the pouch. His hunter used rounds of the same caliber as the short repeater he and Kard now both wielded, but the cartridges and the rounds themselves were longer.

Tyrus was right that he *could* fire the repeater rounds through his hunter in an emergency. It wasn't safe or efficient, but it might be useful. Maybe.

"We'll stick to the repeaters, I think," Kard observed. "Thank you, old friend."

"Tyrus regrets Tyrus not able to teach Teer more," the shaman said. "Tyrus not know if the teaching helps as much as Kard hoped, but there was more *to* teach."

Teer finished placing his saddle on Star and began attaching the long scabbards for his weapons. Star was used to the hunter hanging on the one side, but she whinnied a touch as he hung the repeater and the saber opposite it.

"It's okay, girl," he murmured to her, stroking her neck. "Thank you, Tyrus," he continued to the shaman. "I...I think I learned some useful things. I'll keep working on 'em."

The biggest thing he figured he'd picked up from Tyrus was simple: to do anything at his full supernatural speed, he needed to learn to do it at a far more sedate pace and then speed it up over time.

Slow is learning. Learning is skill. Skill is speed.

"Teer understands," Tyrus concluded. "Teer's heart is in right place, sense of honor solid. Follow Kard. Remind Kard, time of times, that *Kard's* heart is in right place. And that Kard should take counsel of heart, not of fear."

"I am standing right here," Kard observed drily.

"And Tyrus has told Kard this before," the shaman said. "So, Tyrus reminds Teer to remind Kard. Be guardian, as Kard once promised. Not refugee, as Kard's fear counsels."

There was a long silence.

"You know what hunts me," Kard said quietly. "You know what is written."

"Tyrus knows Kard fears tablets of stone and the words of Kard's father." The shaman shrugged. "Kota prophecy...messier. Tyrus figures if Spehari prophecy so powerful, Unity be even stronger than it is!"

Kard chuckled sadly.

"Prophecy is rarely easy, straightforward or even *useful*," he admitted. "But when it's clear, it's clear enough. The King in Winter uses what he has, and it's part of *why* the Unity is as strong as it is."

Teer had no idea what the two men were talking about, though Kard had once told him that the El-Spehari's fate was "written on tablets of stone."

"For now, a different hunt awaits us," Kard concluded. "Teer, is there anything you need to do before we leave?"

Teer had finished adding the pouches of blessed bullets to each of their saddlebags. Both horses were loaded up—the only thing that wasn't definitely ready was the two men who would ride them.

And he knew what Kard was asking about.

"Better, I think, if not."

His boss studied him, then gestured for them to mount up.

"Better to let a thing end and be fondly remembered," Kard told him, "than to destroy it fighting to preserve it."

The El-Spehari chuckled at Teer's surprised look.

"I cannot sire children and will outlive all friends not of Spehari blood," he pointed out. "The El-Spehari have always known our nature. So, we have lived and loved grandly and vividly."

"And tragically."

Tyrus's words finished Kard's thought in a very different tone than Kard had used, but the El-Spehari nodded.

"And tragically," he agreed. "As I said, we know our nature. We will meet again, Tyrus. Not this turning, perhaps, but before either of us leaves this world."

"Is that carved in Spehari tablets of stone?" Tyrus asked archly.

"No. *That* is a promise of mine."

6

Getting out of the Venedor Hills proved easier than getting in. For one thing, this time, Teer and Kard were on their own, and while Lora had been willing enough and tough enough, she'd been a townswoman until recently.

For another, they weren't looking for a hidden town this time. They were keeping an eye out for the callipsuses, but their actual route was straightforward enough: straight west.

Evening fell just as they reached the edge of the hills, where the smaller rises rolled smoothly into the vast plains that defined the eastern limits of the Unity. Out on those plains, somewhere, was the ranch Teer had grown up on.

Somewhere out there was the cattle drive his stepfather had tried to find him a place amongst, too. In hindsight, Teer could see the effort and the hope Hardin had put into that thought—though at the time it had contributed to the anger that had resulted in him *shooting* Kard.

Not all lessons were learned cheaply.

"I don't see any water," he told Kard. "But we should be thinking about camping for the night to protect the horses' hooves."

"I know," the El-Spehari agreed. He rose up in his stirrups, which between Kard's own height and Clack's extra shoulders over Star probably gave him another four or five inches of altitude to search from.

"I was hoping there'd be something," Kard admitted. "Where there's farms and ranches, there's *something* resembling roads—and those tend to lead toward water. But I think we're still well outside anything the Unity claims."

Teer snorted bitterly as he slowed Star up.

"Is there anything the Unity doesn't *claim*?" he asked.

"Whatever's west of the Sea of Storms," Kard said seriously. He pulled Clack up as well and sighed.

"Water the horses first," he instructed. "This isn't a particularly dry area, so we should find something tomorrow, but we'll look to their needs and then ours. No rehydrated stews tonight."

Teer chuckled.

"We're on *Lora's* version of those now," he warned. They still had a small stash of his mother's supplies, made with love and potentially magic, but those would keep forever, in his experience. Preserving them was important.

Lora's version wasn't…*bad*. It just didn't stack up to Alana's at all.

"Which are fine," Kard replied, clearly following Teer's trail of thought. "But it's Kotan trailbread tonight."

"Ah."

Teer had packed the leaf-wrapped loaves of trailbread with trepidation. Alana did her best to take care of the cattlehands, but he'd eaten trailbread before. Baked hard enough to make staleness irrelevant, it wasn't the most pleasant of meals.

But maybe the Kotan version would surprise him. Stranger things had happened.

To Teer's surprise, Kard still lit a small fire once they had the horses settled. The El-Spehari spent a few minutes poking through his supplies and the surrounding area until he eventually came back with a flat rock, slightly larger than a dinner plate but much thicker.

"Watch and learn," Kard told the younger man as he pulled out their usual cauldron stand and used it to suspend the stone above the fire.

The wires and so forth weren't quite up to the task, Teer judged, but the flickers of blue light around Kard's hands told him the older hunter was using magic to stabilize his impromptu stovetop.

"Now grab me a couple of the trailbreads," Kard ordered. "Each should be a decent meal on its own, but we can toast another if we're still hungry after."

In Teer's experience, toasting hardtack didn't make much difference. Still, he found two of the leaf-wrapped packages and proffered them to his boss. To his further surprise, Kard just tossed the two loaves onto the hot stone without removing the redgrave leaves.

"The leaves are edible," he observed. "And it adds some useful flavor to them, too. Now we wait a bit and listen."

"Listen?" Teer asked. He was more used to judging how done food was by steam and temperature.

"You'll see," Kard replied. He tucked his legs under himself, sitting cross-legged by the fire and staring into it. Purple sparks of light flickered off him as he did, scattering out around their tiny camp to form a rough circle.

"Magic?"

His boss nodded.

"Alarms," Kard said. "I don't *think* the callipsuses are going to be hunting us specifically, but you *did* put several bullets through their middle child. Nia killed it, but you hurt it."

Teer sighed.

"So, its parents hate me specifically," he noted.

"Likely," his boss replied. "I don't know much about parenting. My father was...well, a Spehari Lord with neither time nor emotion to spare on his halfblood child. I was an *investment* far more than I was his child.

"But at that, I think my father *still* would have burned down half the Unity to avenge me." Kard shrugged. "And callipsuses don't really have a society, as I understand it, to require them to hide their emotions. They are very intelligent and magically powerful but not social outside their family groupings.

"Probably because they can eat *each other's* brains to reproduce, too," he concluded thoughtfully.

Further conversation was interrupted by an odd sizzling sound from the heated stone.

"Good. Grab the plates," Kard instructed.

He shifted one of the loaves onto a plate for Teer and smiled.

"Give it a few heartbeats to cool, then eat it as is," he instructed.

Teer obeyed and was...pleasantly surprised. The trailbread was probably better than regular trailbread on its own, with nuts and dried fruit and meat baked into it. It was fresh enough that it might even have been soft on its own, but the leaf-wrapping had almost melted into the loaf, adding an icing-like layer that softened the bread.

It was still a reheated chunk of bread with dehydrated fruits and meat, but it was more palatable than a lot of rations he'd eaten while out with the cattle.

"Told you," Kard said. He'd already inhaled over half of his.

Teer nodded his concession around a bite of bread, staring blankly into the fire as he continued to eat. Finally, his meal done, he glanced over at Kard.

"You keep talking about tablets of stone and prophecy," he murmured. "I feel like there's something you know is coming. I'm supposed to protect you. Storms, I have the distinct impression that your dyin' would be bad for me! I think I deserve to know what you think is coming."

There was a long silence around the campfire, then the El-Spehari nodded.

"Aye, fair enough," he allowed. "So far as I know, you should survive something happening to me. Few unpleasant days, but it shouldn't kill you. Given how much you resist mind magic, you might not even get that."

"Fair." Teer had resisted several pieces of Kard's magic when they'd met and the El-Spehari had tried to compel truth from him. They were *alive* because he was equally resistant to the illusion powers of the callipsuses.

"But if you think something is going to be killing you..."

"As I said, fair enough," Kard repeated. "Just...considering the beginning."

Teer nodded, cleaning up the plates while his boss sorted through his thoughts.

"First," Kard finally began, "you have to realize that when I speak of stone tablets of prophecy, it is not a metaphor. The Thousand Tablets came on the iron ships from the west. They arrived in Aran with my father's people."

Teer had been given a couple of books to read in jail. One of them had been *A History of the Spehari Unification, Volume I: Landings and the Merik*. While it included basically no information about where the Spehari had come to the continent of Aran *from*, it had been clear that they had come from somewhere out west, carried upon ships built of iron that had been melted down to build the Iron Pillars.

Teer wasn't entirely sure what the Iron Pillars *were*, though the story was that the King in Winter had killed the Prince in Sunset beneath them—and his capital city *was* called the City of the Pillars. At least some of the Iron Pillars had to be there.

Plus, they were scattered up and down the coast. He didn't remember it well, but the fishing village he'd been born in had grown up around one of them. He knew what an Iron Pillar *looked* like.

He just didn't know what they were.

"As it was explained to me in my schooling, there are actually about seventeen hundred tablets," Kard continued with a soft chuckle. "They're called the Thousand Tablets because roughly a thousand of them had been carved when the Spehari arrived here.

"The others were blank. There is some property of the stone of the tablets itself that enables the prophetic powers the Spehari wield. They cannot be erased or reused. Once a Tablet has been carved, that is a measure of the Unity's ability to predict the future gone forever."

He shrugged, still staring into the fire.

"Interpreting them is more an art than a skill," he murmured. "There are...names that appear in them that have never been given to any living child. Names such as *King in Winter*. *Prince in Sunset*."

Teer recognized those names. They'd seemed odd to him, but the

Spehari *were* odd. Demigods who walked among more mortal peoples, with powers and knowledge none of their subjects could match.

"Or." Kard looked away from the fire to meet Teer's gaze. "The Warlord and the Child of the Rising Bloom." He smiled sadly. "'Rising bloom' is what *Morais* means, my friend. I am—as far as I know—the youngest child of the House of the Rising Bloom and, as 'the Child of the Rising Bloom,' I am in the Thousand Tablets."

"You've seen 'em?" Teer asked.

"Iron Pillars, no." Kard chuckled. "Many of the original Thousand Tablets speak to things before we came east. Some of those are forever sealed. Others are only allowed to the King in Winter himself. Others, though, can be studied by some of the senior Spehari.

"And my father is *very* senior. So, he has, as I understand it, seen every Tablet that references the Rising Bloom. Enough for him to be certain that the 'Warlord of the Rising Bloom' refers to him. By Spehari tradition, he could in fact claim that title."

Kard was looking right through Teer, as if he was staring into a distance only he could see.

"But if Lord Akane of House Morais formally accepted that he was the Warlord of the Rising Bloom, then that would be the last piece of matching events to make *me* the *Child* of the Rising Bloom," Kard said softly. "And that would have tied into all kinds of prophecies around rebellion and lies and blood."

He shrugged.

"I knew some of this before the Sunset Rebellion," he observed. "The Prince in Sunset knew more. He was, so far as I know, the only El-Spehari ever allowed into the Hall of the Thousand Tablets.

"But he was special, for all that it was secret. The King in Winter's own grandson, long-prophesied. A shame that some prophecies only become clear after they come true."

"Like his rebellion. And the King killing him," Teer guessed.

"I think that if the King in Winter had known how quickly the prophesied events around the Prince in Sunset would occur, and what the final story would be..." Kard blinked away something and sighed.

"I don't know what he would have done, but I can't see him letting things shake out as they did. The Prince in Sunset and the King in

Winter truly were grandson and grandfather, in a way I don't feel my own father and I were. And yet the Prince rebelled and the King killed him."

"And you?" Teer asked.

"It is Written, upon the Thousand Tablets, carved into the stone of our homeland, that the Warlord of the Rising Bloom shall meet the Child of the Rising Bloom in the shade of the Pillars.

"And only one will survive."

Teer exhaled a long sigh.

"And your father?" he asked quietly.

"Is now the Lord Inquisitor," Kard warned. "The Spehari tasked with finding the El-Spehari who have not accepted the Midnight Proclamation. The man tasked with policing magic use in the Unity.

"And while I do believe my father *does* see me as his son, in his own way, I am now everything he is sworn to destroy." The El-Spehari sighed. "So, I will never go anywhere near the Iron Pillars. The far east, a thousand miles and more from those artifacts of Spehari magic, must forever be my home.

"I do not believe I can kill my father. I *do* believe that, regardless of his emotions, my father can kill me. So, I will avoid the Iron Pillars until the day I die."

"Can prophecy be averted like that?" Teer asked.

"Maybe. It depends." Kard spread his hands. "Prophecy is always incomplete and usually vague. The Prince in Sunset may have misread the identifiers for the Child of the Rising Bloom. It might not be me.

"Or it might be me but something must happen first. The prophecies of the Thousand Tablets aren't...fixed. They often take the form of *if this happens, then this will follow*."

"But not enough clarity to prevent the Rebellions."

"No. And I'm told the King in Winter understands them better than anyone else alive." Kard sighed. "So, either even the wisest of the Spehari can get it very wrong—or the alternatives he saw to allowing his grandson to rebel were worse."

Teer sighed and nodded, watching the last coals die down. But Kard's last words raised a question.

"Worse for *who*?"

7

———————

eer's sleep was restless, with strange dreams haunting him through the night. He was familiar, now, with the type of dreams that relived horrific moments. These were something different, with the constant of a strange presence in each of them.

The stranger was *different* across his dreams, but there was a stranger in them all. It was a unfamiliar common thread, one that left him weary and distracted in the morning.

A long ride didn't leave much space for either of those things. He focused on the prairie around them, feeling the warmth of the midmorning sun as he listened for the sound of water.

"That way," he told Kard, gesturing toward the northwest. "I think I hear a spring."

"And here I was about to mention that I *can* do magic to find water," his boss replied with a chuckle. "Your ears have more uses than you think."

Kard urged Clack up to a trot, following Teer toward the water.

The sound led them to much what Teer was expecting: a small rise in the plains where a tiny stream bubbled out from the ground, flowing away toward the north like most water there.

His boss stopped the horses a few yards back, dismounting to pull a water-test crystal from the saddlebags. Teer joined Kard on the ground, holding the horses as the older man tested the water.

"Crystal says it's clear," Kard reported. "I'll fill the canteens; you water the horses downstream?"

———

EVEN WITH THEIR water supplies replenished, the pair followed the stream for the rest of the morning. It drifted toward the north and west, merging with several other streams as the water made its way north to the Great Swamp.

Teer heaved an unconcealed sigh of relief when, just as the sun reached high noon, they came across a clearly marked ford over the brook. The stone pillars on the sides were crude, but they were standard Unity markings—and the path toward the southwest was clearly worn by hooves and carts.

Not *many* of either, but enough to make it followable.

"Civilization, I guess," Teer said softly.

"Oh, far from civilization," Kard chuckled. "You grew up on the coast, right? Not in Alvid?"

"Sort of." The young Merik looked to the west thoughtfully. "We moved to Alvid when I was all of…eight turnings? Maybe? I don't remember. After the Unity took away Ma's pension."

That had been a "paperwork mix-up," as Teer understood it. Someone had lost the records that said his father had served in the Unity Army, which meant that his widow and child hadn't been entitled to the pension they'd received.

The only thing their local authority had been able to do was prevent the Unity trying to *reclaim* the pension Alana had already been paid. And without that income, Teer's mother hadn't been able to stay in their fishing village.

All of which Kard knew, and Teer could feel his regret for asking.

"Fair; sorry."

They turned onto the road in silence for a few passing minutes, then Kard grumbled wordlessly, staring down at the road.

"*Civilization*," he growled.

"Kard?"

"The City of the Pillars is civilization," Kard replied. "Half a million people, from every tribe the Spehari have 'unified,' in houses of brick and stone along the inlet where the Spehari landed. Towers holding a hundred families, all serving factories that produce the arms and engines of the Unity.

"Alvid is a mill town and a cattle town. A wardtown, guarded by Spehari magic. A fishing village on the coast was…under one of the Iron Pillars, I presume? They serve the same purpose as a wardstone—to the town underneath them, at least.

"But you've never seen the cities of the coast. The city around the Court of Pillars is the greatest, but your people had built mighty towns before my father's people ever came. The Zeeanans did the same to the north and the Rolin to the south.

"All of them are…crowded, noisy, dirty. With your heightened senses, you'd hate them," Kard concluded with a chuckle. "That is what the Unity calls *civilization*."

Teer waited for the second part of what Kard was thinking, recognizing that his boss wasn't done talking.

"If you break a leg in that 'civilization,' you'd better hope you have a contract with someone that says they have to take care of you," the El-Spehari said grimly. "The Spehari Houses *usually* put that in their contracts. Mostly because they see their people as property."

"They aren't wrong, as I hear it."

"No," Kard allowed. "Spehari own everything and everyone. But there's degrees of slavery, I suppose."

Kard's rant was still bouncing on Teer's sore spots, but he simply listened. This was something the El-Spehari needed to get off his chest.

"Even in the farms and ranches, if someone breaks a leg, their neighbors will step in. In places like Alvid, the Wardkeeper often handles an informal pool of funds to help out." Kard shook his head. "The Unity doesn't officially approve, but the Magistrates don't do anything.

"Among the Kota, the shamans handle that kind of thing. Food, healing magic, whatever they think is needed. No one goes uncared-for. But the Kota are not 'civilized' to the Unity."

"That's why I'm out here," Teer observed softly. "Ma couldn't survive on the coast without the widow's pension. Had to find work out east."

"It shouldn't be that way. But to the Spehari…everyone who is not Spehari is a *tool*. And tools that break get replaced."

Teer shivered at Kard's cold words.

"Was that…what the Prince was fighting against?" he asked.

"That was the cause, the story we told everyone," Kard replied. "Some of us believed it more than others. In the end, it didn't matter. To make any changes, we needed to be in control. There were definitely some of my fellow Lord Colonels who were in it for power.

"I think the Prince himself really did want to make things better—but he was going to make himself ruler of the Unity along the way."

Kard sighed.

"People aren't just one thing, Teer," he warned. "Just like a callipsus isn't an animal, a Spehari or a Merik or an El-Spehari… They can be many things at once. Some of those things will conflict with each other.

"The Prince in Sunset, the Governor of the Sunset Provinces… Abarra…" Kard paused thoughtfully. "He wanted to help people, but he also wanted power for its own sake, I think."

"You knew him well?" Teer asked.

"Better, I think, than anyone else ever did," Kard admitted. "Though now that we begin to enter Unity lands, I should conceal myself once more. There are things we cannot speak of, even around those who mean us no harm."

Teer felt a moment of pain as Kard wrapped illusions around himself. Teer could, if he focused, see the image of an even burlier Merik man mounted on Clack.

But without *trying*, he didn't even register that Kard's illusions existed. Spehari mind magic just slid right past Teer's head. That could get him in trouble if he wasn't careful, but it could also be very, very useful.

"This road *should* lead to Shellsvan," Kard said. "We'll probably want to find a farm or some such to stop at for the night. Pay for shelter and a warm meal we don't have to cook."

"Not have to split watches over the night?" Teer asked. "I'm already missing getting a full night's sleep."

It was easier to handle half-and-half watches when he was sleeping well, he'd admit.

"Depends on how trustworthy the folk feel," Kard admitted. "But yeah, I'm hoping for that, too."

8

eer had a moment of almost-painful familiarity as they rode up the rough track toward the fenced farmyard. It wasn't *quite* the same as Hardin's ranch, but he could see the similarities where the rancher had either learned in the same school as Teer's stepfather or followed the same designs.

Given that a lot of ranchers were former cattle-drive hands who would have spent time in the same assortments of mill towns and small cities at the end of the steam-dragon lines, both were easily accurate.

But given the same tools and the same needs, Teer could also see how just about anyone would end up with the same arrangement. A square fenced area, large enough to hold most if not all of the cattle herd with dirt and wooden slats stacked high enough to stand off most predators. A tall square tower by the gate, to allow a watcher to see anything the fences wouldn't hold off—and to find any cattle that strayed! The largest structure was the barn, sized for the smaller winter herd, and the second-largest was a row of small dwellings, not quite houses, for the senior hands.

The rancher's own home would be the third-largest structure, but it would double as the communal kitchen and administration center as well as home for the owner, his wife and their family—potentially including siblings and older parents, depending on the ranch.

Everything about this ranch—hundreds of miles as birds flew from Hardin's, let alone the roundabout route Teer had taken to get there—was familiar to Teer.

Except that this one was deathly silent in the fading light.

"Hello, the tower!" Kard shouted up. "We're a pair of travelers, looking for safe shelter for a night. We've shards to pay for food, even if all the lodging you've got is hay in the barn!"

The pair of them had a number of the redcrystal "stones" used as the anchor for Unity currency. Teer hadn't seen many of those of his own until he'd joined Kard's service. Shards, blue glass coins backed by the Unity rather than any inherent value, were far more common coinage for most people.

But something about the farmyard made Teer suspect they wouldn't need coin tonight. As Kard dismounted and walked forward, Teer drew the short repeater and laid the gun across his knees. Things were *not* right.

"No one in the tower," Kard called back. "Might be a quiet night?"

"No cattle in the yard," Teer replied, kneeing Star forward. "Might be in the barn, but it doesn't smell like it. I...I don't hear *anything*, Kard."

And if the cattle were ranging, there should *definitely* be someone in the tower to keep an eye out for them. Worse, Teer had lived in a ranch yard like this for over ten turnings.

This kind of place was *never* actually quiet.

"Let's see if the gate is locked," Kard told him. "I'll apologize for intruding if I must, but I'd rather help if it's needed!"

———

BOTH OF THEM knew they were too late to provide any help. By the time Teer dismounted in the center of the compound, he *knew* everyone was gone. He could hear people breathe, after all, and no one in the farm buildings was breathing except him and Kard.

There were none of the chickens, pigs or favored milk cows that should have been present in the main compound. The hard-packed ground didn't show tracks well, but Teer was grimly certain what had happened there.

"Would this have been one of the farms Sho scouted?" he asked Kard.

"We're almost a full two days' ride from the Venedors," Kard pointed out. "That's farther than Sho would have scouted. These folk weren't much risk to the Kota. Or, well, to anybody."

Teer stretched his senses, listening and looking to try and locate anything…and then the smell hit him.

"Oh."

His boss looked at him questioningly.

"I smell death," Teer said quietly. He checked that the repeater was fully loaded, then dropped Star's reins in the manner she was trained for.

He didn't wait to see if Kard was following him as he set off. To someone with Teer's senses, there was always going to be *some* smell of death in a working ranch yard. Between chickens, pigs, cattle and such, it was rare for a tenday to go by without something being slaughtered.

This was something else and Teer knew it.

"Cartridge casings," Kard pointed out from behind him. Teer followed the thought and looked at the ground. The rancher and their hands hadn't managed anything so dramatic as a barricade or a final stand, but it looked like whatever fighting had happened had occurred in front of the ranch house.

There weren't a lot of casings. A handful of the longer brass cases from hunters. A dozen, maybe two, of the shorter ones for quick-shooters.

"Two shooters with hunters, three with quickshooters," Kard said quietly. "One of the pistoleers had two guns." He paused. "None of them managed to empty the quickshooters, though the two with hunters got a couple of reloads in."

Unlike repeaters or quickshooters, hunters didn't have magazines. They were breechloading weapons, and a skilled user could fire and reload in three, maybe four heartbeats.

"No guns, no bodies…no blood," Teer noted. "No one was killed here."

"I don't like what I think that means," Kard told him.

"Me either. This way." Teer led his boss around the house. There'd been a vegetable garden there, and *that* showed the first tracks they'd seen. Where most of the yard was hard-packed and sunbaked dirt, with a couple of flagstone paths, the garden had been plants and soft soil.

All of which had been disturbed when the bodies were dragged through it. There were no footprints to be seen initially, but Kard pointed as they reached the corner of the house.

Embedded in the soil was a single wide-toed print, utterly inhuman and larger than any bootprint Teer had ever seen.

"Callipsus," Kard said flatly.

"Yeah." Teer stepped around the ranch house and found what had clearly *been* the butcher's station, tucked away from the main yard. Except that where there would have been a small open pit for the unusable animal bits, there was instead a neatly stacked array of corpses.

He swallowed down his gorge at the smell. It should have been worse, but there was very little blood. The bodies were oddly dried out, as if left in far brighter sunshine for weeks or months.

He forced himself to calm, taking a cold few moments to work through the bodies. There were seventeen of them. About half men and women, most Zeeanan, he concluded absently.

It was when he spotted the two children, neither of whom could have been over twelve turnings, that his self-control slipped. He had enough presence left to recognize that *every* skull had been cut open with some kind of blade before he had to flee back around the house and be violently ill.

KARD FOUND him a few moments later, leaning against the house and breathing heavily.

"It's never easy," the El-Spehari said quietly. "I'm hardened to it, I guess, but I don't think that is a good thing. Violence. Blood. Murder. None of it is pretty."

Teer swallowed and nodded.

"That could have been me," he whispered. "And my brother and family. They were folk just like us."

"Yes," Kard agreed. "And for all of your gifts and skills, against a callipsus, unaware? You would have faced a similar fate."

The illusion of a Merik flickered away, leaving behind only the pale-skinned man with the knifelike ears, looking gently at Teer.

"This is why we fight them," he told Teer. "They don't have a choice but to kill and feed on us. *We* don't have a choice but to fight them. They are not evil—men who do things like this are evil, but a callipsus is driven by instinct and need.

"But just because they are not *evil* does not mean we have to stand aside and let them hunt. Like a wolfen or a dragon, we know they do not attack out of ill will. But we stop them anyway."

"You said yourself, they're not animals," Teer pointed out. "They have to *know* this is…wrong."

"They don't have the same values you and I have. They put themselves and their desire to spawn over the lives of strangers." Kard grimaced. "I've known many people of every tribe who would do the same, if less brutally.

"I do not believe callipsuses are evil," he reiterated. "I *do* believe they have to be stopped. I will hunt them, fight them—*destroy* them. Because I will not stand by and watch innocents die.

"But I also believe that we need to understand *why* they do what they do. And recognize that we might well do the same, given the same limitations and drives. We must end them. We must protect the weak around us."

"That is why we are Hunters," Teer said softly. "To protect."

"Yes. And while the callipsuses are not evil, as I would judge it, they are a *danger*. So, we hunt."

Teer wasn't sure he followed Kard's logic—or that he cared, for that matter. There was a level of thinking to Kard's words that was beyond him. Anything that would do what he'd seen behind the house was evil. Regardless of its reasons.

He guessed it didn't matter. He and Kard would both hunt the monsters that had done this.

"I'm going to take care of the bodies," Kard finally told him. "While I don't think either of us feels up to using the *beds* here, go check out the kitchen. If things are in good-enough shape, we can at least make ourselves real food and then bed down under a roof."

9

Even with just their regular bedrolls, setting up in the farmhouse living room gave them cover from the weather and wind that they wouldn't have outside. Teer agreed with Kard, though—he didn't have it in him to use the beds in the house.

He knew it wouldn't change anything. The ranch's people were dead. Using their beds, their kitchen, even their supplies—it wouldn't change anything. If it helped hunt their killers, it might even make *sense.*

But it felt disrespectful. So, Teer wrapped himself in his regular bedroll, tucked against a wall of the farmhouse and managed to drift off to sleep.

His dreams were fitful again, bringing him back to wakefulness several times before he finally drifted off and fell into something more solid.

Somehow, he knew he was dreaming—and that he was also *not.* He was asleep; he knew that. He stood in his mother's kitchen in Hardin's ranch house, so similar to the one he'd just cooked in.

The dream had a sharp clarity he'd rarely felt before, and he could *feel* that something was going on even before the stranger stepped into the room.

A strange scent accompanied the man, like the smell of air after a storm, and he bestowed Teer with a gentle smile as the young Merik tried to understand what was going on.

The stranger was tall, even taller than Teer or Kard. His skin was bronzed and weathered, and his hair was pure white—and a nasty scar crossed his face, twisting his skin to close up his left eye socket.

"Finally," he declared. "I knew I *could* reach you. But your friend's tricks make you hard to touch."

"Who are you?" Teer demanded. Somehow, he knew what was going on. The stranger was a real person, one who was reaching into his dreams by magic.

"My kind don't...have names as you understand them," the stranger replied. "We don't really *speak* like you. This is an interpretation, your mind translating the message I send into forms you understand.

"My name among my own kind is... Well, the concept is most easily spoken as *the scent of air after the storm*." The old man chuckled. "Call me Storm. It's as useful as anything."

"Storm." Teer could smell the being's name around him as he stood in the illusion of his mother's kitchen. "You're the callipsus."

He wasn't sure how he was so certain of that, but he *knew*.

"That is the Spehari word for us, I suppose," Storm agreed. "Our concept is...*the rising hunger of the living minds*." He chuckled. "Like much, it doesn't translate well."

"You killed everyone here," Teer said flatly. "I don't know what you want, *monster*, but I don't think you'll find it here."

Storm smiled and shook his head gently.

"Teer, Teer. Do you truly think the chickens would have been any happier with the scene *we* found than you were? Predators do not choose what they are. Prey does not *want* to be prey.

"But I must feed and spawn and feed my children." He shrugged. "I do not enjoy it. By magic and claw, we make it as painless and clean as we can."

"And that's supposed to make me think your slaughter is acceptable?" Teer demanded. He was surprised that the callipsus could even do this, and he started to try to focus, through his dream, to drive the monster out.

"You killed *my* child. I don't *care* what you think," Storm admitted. "I don't think you have the training to drive me out, young one. More powerful Adepts than you have tried and failed. And you are such a poorly trained little thing, aren't you? Barely worth the effort to break."

Teer wasn't used to his dreams being this…real. Still, he found his old quickshooter hanging at his belt, the gun—broken in the real world—rising smoothly in his hand to fire at Storm.

The one-eyed old man sidestepped the gunfire, shaking his head and clicking his tongue.

"I am not your enemy, Teer," Storm told him. "I might eat you, but I am not your enemy. You're not even…ripe. I have a trade to offer."

"I am not interested."

The scent of storm air strengthened and the callipsus's illusion laughed.

"You may change your mind," Storm told him. "I can *feel* your lack of training, little Adept. I have to wonder. Is there even anyone left to train you, or did the Spehari wipe them all out?"

A chill ran down Teer's spine as he realized Storm was using the label *Adept* for him, specifically. He had no idea what the creature meant, and another chuckle echoed through the dream.

"As I believed. There is no one to train you. You are lost, the Spehari having destroyed all that you could have been."

"Get. Out. Of. My. Head."

Teer was surprised by the power that answered his call, energy surging across his dream as he tried to drive Storm out of his dream.

The callipsus simply laughed at him.

"I can train you," Storm told Teer. "Those we consume are not lost forever, child. I remember everything they knew. I can teach you. I can give you the skills of a fully trained Adept of the Merik Orders, give you the knowledge to use the gifts you already have.

"And in exchange, you will deliver to me what I have never tasted: the mind and soul of an El-Spehari. Deliver this 'Kard' to me, Teer, and

I will restore to you the knowledge and power that the Spehari have denied you."

It turned out that Storm did, in fact, have something Teer wanted. But even if he was prepared to believe that the monster could teach him how to use his gifts, it didn't matter. He wasn't going to betray Kard.

"I cannot," he told the monster, focusing his mental strength again and drawing on his bond with Kard this time. "I have sworn my life and I will not betray him—not to anyone, let alone a monster that eats *children*."

This time, the crash of mental energy shattered the illusion of his mother's kitchen, and Teer bolted upright, finally awake.

Breathing rapidly, he stared blankly at the walls for several moments, wishing he could somehow convince himself it had truly been just a dream.

———

TEER SWALLOWED HIS BREATH, focusing on the plain whitewashed wall, then exhaled slowly. Three heartbeats in. Three heartbeats out. Repeat.

"They're coming," he said softly.

"What?"

Kard had moved a carefully handmade wooden chair over by the door. He'd seated himself, a cup in one hand and his repeater leaning against the side of the chair, keeping watch.

"The callipsuses," Teer told him. "They know where we are. One of 'em tried to talk to me… in my head. In my *dream*."

He shivered. That felt…sick, in a way few things did. Not quite on par with the blood ward being used to steal Lora's life, but in the same vein of just *wrong*.

"Tried to convince me to betray you," Teer told his boss. "In exchange for teachin' me how to be…an Adept, he called it? Of the Merik Orders?"

There was a long silence, then Kard drained whatever was in his cup. The El-Spehari's magic flickered around the room, moving the mug to a side table as he rose to his feet, his gun in his hands.

"I'd wondered about those," he admitted. "They were destroyed while I was a child, and the story by the time I served the Unity was that they had been theoretically religious groups." He sighed. "Ones that had coordinated treasonous activities and plotted against the Unity. Hence their destruction."

"The callipsus... He said he had the memories of everyone he'd eaten and could train me to be an Adept of the Merik Orders," Teer repeated. "And he wanted me to betray you to him in exchange for that.

"I don't see why he'd've wanted to confuse and distract us like that unless they were *here*. Ready to strike."

"Agreed."

Teer picked up his own repeater and belted on his quickshooters. Even in the middle of the night, it was warm enough that he was hesitant to put on the armored greatcoat.

The image in his mind of the carved-open skulls pushed him to anyway.

"What are you thinking?" Teer asked Kard.

"They will attempt illusions, trying to separate us," the El-Spehari concluded softly. "If they know that you're resistant, they will focus on me."

Kard rummaged through his things as he spoke and removed a clay jar with a screw top attached. He carefully opened it, scooping a red-tinged lotion out with his fingers and rubbing it into his eyes.

Blinking against something, he offered the ointment to Teer.

"Tyrus made this for me, to bar the callipsuses' illusions," he explained. "On you, it should render you completely immune to their mind power. The difference might not be huge, but if we are outnumbered by creatures that are superior to us one-on-one, I'll take what I can get."

Teer nodded and took the jar. The lotion stung for a few moments after he applied it, forcing him to blink and mix tears in with the ointment.

The stinging faded, replaced by a warm sensation that suggested the magic was working. He closed the jar and stepped over to the door with Kard.

"The building is solid," he observed. "I think it'd stop gunfire, even, and they don't have guns. Right?"

"They don't need them," Kard said grimly. "Not when they can mess with people's heads and have claws that can go through most armor. But if we can see them coming…"

The El-Spehari smiled.

"Let's block off the doors and check the shutters throughout. I don't think the locks will cut it on their own, but with a bit of work, we can make their life difficult.

"And the longer it takes them to get in, the more time we have to shoot them."

10

The farmhouse didn't have a great many windows, only one in most rooms, and all of them had solid wooden shutters. Teer wasn't sure that the shutters would hold up on their own, but he also saw the blue glitter of Kard's magic reinforcing them.

The same blue glitter wrapped around the two side doors and the heavy furniture Teer had moved across them. Bars and locks and magic and dressers left him reasonably certain the callipsuses wouldn't be able to break through the side doors.

He supposed they could even have closed and sealed the windows from the living room and waited for dawn. Neither of them had even suggested it. They were heading west to try to hunt down these monsters, so an opportunity to take them on from a fortified position seemed worth it to Teer!

Secondmoon had set and thirdmoon barely rose that night, plunging the farmyard and the surrounding plains into a darkness sparsely lit by stars. Kard was more on edge once secondmoon had set, and Teer was right with him.

If the callipsuses were going to come, they'd come in the darkness.

Each of the two Hunters had taken a spot by a window overlooking the main homestead yard and the hard-packed path connecting the ranch to the main road.

The first sign that they were not alone was a soft pressure building up in the back of Teer's head. He shivered and glanced over at Kard.

"Seeing anything strange?" he asked.

"No…why?"

"Feeling the edge of what could be a headache," Teer replied. "It feels like that cave where we met the first one, but without the pain."

"Then I guess Tyrus's ointment worked," Kard murmured. "I don't see anything. Can you… You can see illusions you're piercing if you try, can't you?"

Teer nodded slowly, then *focused* as he did when he was trying to see Kard's illusions.

"There," he said, pointing out toward the road where shapes of orange sparks now danced across his vision. "Looks like it's supposed to be a wagon and riders, but they aren't hiding *in* the illusion."

The outline of orange lights approached the gate and seemed to go through the same motions Teer and Kard had of trying to speak to someone in the watch tower. Teer couldn't see the source of the illusion, but he focused on where they *had* to be.

A patch of shadow seemed to shift as the illusory travelers approached the gate. A callipsus moved in the night, opening the gate in concert with the illusions and then moving into the yard slowly.

The illusions moved in more quickly. As Teer focused, he could barely make out voices calling toward the house, asking if there was anyone home able to offer warmth to weary travelers.

"One in the middle of the illusion," Teer murmured. "Hard to get a sense of them, though."

Even seeing through the callipsuses' magic, he was struggling to pick out their mottled gray-green skin in the dark. The creatures knew how to move without being seen, even though they were relying on their illusions for a distraction.

"Let's try *this*."

Kard's words were accompanied by a bolt of blue that flashed up into the sky above the farm. About a hundred feet into the air, the magic burst into a light that Teer figured *everyone* could see.

Probably for miles in every direction, at that. The farmyard was lit up as clear as day, and Teer could now see his enemy.

A moment after that, he really wished he *couldn't*. The closest of the three creatures advancing across the farmyard seemed to be glaring right at him, its eyes massive black orbs rapidly blinking in the sudden light.

The creatures were *immense*. The juvenile he'd fought before had been as tall as he was, with a long tail, but he could see now how undeveloped that one had been. The one whose gaze he was unexpectedly meeting was easily the height of two men—and half again as long as it was tall.

It was definitely a lizard, though it strode upright on its hind legs and its arms looked more person-like than he expected. Wicked-looking sickle-shaped claws clicked on the flagstones of the path approaching the house, and sharp teeth the size of knives flashed in Kard's artificial sunlight.

Teer fired. Eight shots *cracked* out across the yard in six heartbeats, each of them one of Tyrus's blessed bullets that should have pierced even callipsus skin. Four shots at the closest, two at each of the others.

He did not normally miss. Against human enemies, eight shots would have been overkill.

The callipsuses moved with alien grace, twisting like they had snakes instead of torsos. None of Teer's bullets hit, a third of his magical ammunition wasted as the creatures moved like no enemy he'd ever seen.

Kard fired a moment after Teer, his shots ringing out at one a heartbeat and his fire focused on the lead callipsus.

None of those bullets hit either, and the three reptilian monsters charged. It was only as the smell hit Teer's thoughts, the *scent of air after the storm*, that he recognized the largest of the creatures. Fourteen feet tall to the other two callipsuses' twelve, the being was missing one of its eyes.

The same eye as Storm had been missing in the dream—and Teer suspected that he wasn't *smelling* anything.

Even as he was processing Storm's presence, his fingers were loading bullets into the repeater's magazine. The creatures had crossed almost the entirety of the farmyard by the time even *he* had finished reloading, and he snapped the gun back up as the lead callipsus reached the front of the house.

A massively powerful leg as large as he was tall crashed into the front door. Wood splintered, but Teer saw Kard's magic flare bright blue and hold the entrance together.

And for a moment, the massive lizard was stuck against the door. Teer put three bullets into the creature's raised leg before it recovered, and two more into its torso before it twisted around the remaining three rounds of his fusillade.

It still seemed at least a touch stunned—but Teer hadn't loaded with Tyrus's rounds this time. He'd hit it—hard—but it was still upright, and now both of the smaller monsters were charging toward his window.

A bolt of red light flashed past his head, leaving a trail of warmth across the side of his skull, and took the lead callipsus in the center of its torso, twisting with the creature as it tried to dodge. The callipsus found itself lifted from the ground and flung back a dozen feet.

The second unleashed an inhumanly fast kick, a massive claw slashing toward Teer's face—but he grabbed one of his quickshooters in the momentary cover of Kard's magical attack. The guns he'd taken from a dead Hunter were masterpieces of the gunsmith's art, among the few arms he'd met that could withstand his full speed.

Five shots rang out so close together that even *Teer* only heard them as one crescendo of fire. He saw the claw snap under the impacts—and *heard* the callipsus's leg, already battered by his last rounds, break.

The one Kard had thrown back was skittering away on all fours, its tail straight out behind it to balance a turn of speed Teer would never have expected from the massive creature. Storm appeared to have just...disappeared at some point, which was worrying.

And the last callipsus clearly realized it wasn't going to be able to run with a broken leg. Pivoting on its uninjured leg, it smashed its tail into the wall of the farmhouse with enough force to break brick and wood alike. The window would never have been large enough for the callipsus to enter, but the hole it smashed through the walls—walls sturdy enough to stop *bullets*—was enough larger that Teer wasn't certain.

"Teer! Catch!"

Kard's repeater flashed across the room, and Teer snatched it out of the air. There was no time for him to check how many bullets were in it —or whether it was loaded with Tyrus's rounds or regular cartridges.

The callipsus crashed through the hole it had made in the wall. Teer might have broken its leg and one of its claws, but it had a *lot* of claws left—and teeth—all of which were heading straight at his face.

He caught the biting muzzle with the tip of the gun, using his strength and the massive creature's own speed to swing it around onto the ground. More of the wall gave way under the callipsus's weight as it smashed down, and Teer had a clean shot at the top of the monster's mouth.

There were three bullets in the gun, it turned out, and Teer put all three perfectly into the top of the callipsus's jaw. All three exploded out the top of the creature's head in a spray of red-gray gore, marking that the gun *had* been loaded with the blessed bullets.

The monster spasmed massively, its flailing tail finishing the job of wrecking the wall it had broken through, and then was suddenly still.

"Watch for the others," Kard barked. "Reload!"

Teer tossed Kard's repeater back, the El-Spehari snatching it out of the air with a flash of magic, and grabbed his own weapon.

Eight cartridges slid home in four heartbeats, and he found himself using the callipsus's corpse as cover. It was still warm, the scales strangely slick as he propped the gun on the body, surveying the yard lit by Kard's magic.

"I can't see either of them," Teer said softly. "There's a bit of a trail where the one ran, but Storm is just…gone."

"Storm was the big one?" Kard asked. "The one who entered your dream?"

"Yeah. The one-eyed one," Teer confirmed.

"I haven't heard of any of them getting that big," his boss told him. "And one eye…"

Kard surveyed the yard silently, a second pulse of power augmenting the light.

"I think we've run them off," he noted slowly. "Do me a favor?"

"Sure." Kard literally *owned* Teer, in more senses than one, but Teer appreciated that his boss treated him as a junior partner, not a magically bound servant.

"Take that Kott-steel saber I gave you and cut that thing's head off," Kard ordered. "I don't want to wake up in the morning and find another one of these monsters has wandered off after we thought it was dead.

"Plus, I have a use for a callipsus head. It will make a good chunk of my plan a *lot* easier."

11

By the time the sun dawned palely over the northern prairie, Teer was hopeful that the two remaining callipsuses were going to keep their distance. Still, one of the pair of Hunters stayed alert at all times—with a repeater loaded with Tyrus's blessed bullets to hand.

Teer's main focus had been finding a bag to put the severed head in. Searching through the farmhouse, it was clear to him that this had been a prosperous and thriving little community before Storm had arrived.

The animals had clearly been scared off by the monsters who'd killed their people, but the presence of wool and tanned hides told him they'd been raising both sheep and cattle—the former were uncommon on the eastern edge of the Unity, but Teer had known some shepherds.

Unlike Hardin's farm, there was a very limited amount of machine-woven cloth or other items brought from back west. This ranch had been significantly more self-sufficient than the one Teer had grown up on, but they'd been in some ways *more* prosperous for that.

The storeroom full of cloth made there didn't include any bags, though he eventually found a burlap sack large enough for the callipsus's oversized head and wrapped the grotesque trophy up.

"Wash your hands," Kard told him as he finished sealing the bag. "Then take over watch as I deal with the rest of the body."

The callipsuses had made a mess of the exterior of the house, Teer realized as he walked a brisk patrol around the yard, gun in hand. The structures hadn't shown much wear when they'd arrived—like the state of the bodies Teer had found, that suggested the original attack hadn't been too long before.

It had, he suspected, been long enough before that the callipsuses had specifically returned to the homestead to ambush them. That was an uncomfortable thought, but Teer brushed it aside to focus on the task at hand.

The ease with which Kard magically dug graves was concerning. He hadn't noticed when they'd dealt with the Hunters the previous tenday, but now it chafed at his nerves. His El-Spehari boss had clearly done this before—a *lot*.

The callipsus corpse was big enough and heavy enough that Kard used more magic to roll it into the deep pit he'd carved, before filling the dirt back in and looking back at Teer with a sigh.

"I feel like we're doing these people a disservice just leaving the place like this, but I don't know what else to do," he admitted.

"Time'll wreck it," Teer agreed sadly. "The damage we and the callipsuses did to the house won't help. But short of movin' in, nothing we can do'll fix it. Storm and his kin killed this place in every way. There's nothing we can do. Much as I wish we could."

His boss grimaced and nodded.

"I buried the folk from here last night," he told Teer. "It's…easier on me to handle that kind of thing. I've seen worse."

There was a long silence.

"It's not something you can get used to, but you can learn to handle it," Kard concluded. "I hope that you never have to. It's…" He sighed with another grimace. "It's *war* that teaches you that, and I don't plan on leading you into one of those."

"You said yourself that the fight against the callipsuses was basically a war," Teer countered. "And after this place...I'll fight 'em. Wherever we find 'em."

"Aye." Kard stared off into space for a few more moments, then shrugged and called his illusory self back into place.

"Let's grab the horses and get going. We're still a couple of days from Shellsvan—and the sooner we find the Unity troops, the less that head is going to stink."

TEER SPENT the entire day twitching at every movement in the long grass, every animal that ran over the prairie. He didn't think that the callipsuses could catch up at speed without him hearing and seeing them coming, but the previous night had left him worried.

So did the heavy bag tied to his saddle that was making Star uncomfortable. There was an acrid smell to it, unlike anything he'd ever dealt with before, and the mare definitely didn't like it.

Neither did Teer, for that matter, but he could live with it.

"How many of Tyrus's bullets do we have left?" Kard asked him around midday. "I've got a full load in my magazine and four rounds left."

"I have two full loads, I think," Teer replied. "Guess I should pass you a couple so we've the same amount?"

"I'm actually thinking about giving you all of them," the El-Spehari admitted. "I have my own ways of hurting them, but you are limited to the Kott-steel saber and Tyrus's bullets."

Teer thought it over.

"The saber will hurt them?" he asked.

"The Kott made it for one of my fellow Lord Colonels," Kard told him. "They made one for each of us, and I picked up Sirak's when she was killed. I don't pretend to understand the different grades of Kott iron and steel, but these swords were the same they forged for their own princes."

He snorted.

"A Kott prince told me that they forged these blades so that if a prince had to choose between his people and the gods, he carried a blade that could cut the gods."

Teer considered the phrase for a few moments as they considered along the trail.

"That makes the expectation pretty clear, doesn't it?" he finally asked. "You have one of these too?"

"I actually have *two* more," Kard admitted. "The Kott made us fifteen and, well, I don't think any of the other Lord Colonels survived."

Teer wasn't entirely sure *where* Kard had two more swords tucked away in his saddlebags, though he was learning that Clack was very efficiently packed. They kept acquiring extra horses from people who tried to kill them, and then selling or giving the animals away.

He figured they could use a packhorse, but somehow, Kard kept making it work. He suspected there was more magic woven into Kard's things than the El-Spehari even *remembered*, let alone admitted to.

"I guess it makes sense for me t' have the bullets, then," he agreed. "If you're sure? What if you have to fight one and keep up your illusions?"

The silence was only broken by hoofbeats for a good minute before his boss sighed.

"Seas take it, you're right," Kard said. "We're looking for one of my kin and the troops they'll have brought with them. I can't afford to lower my illusions and use my power to fight the callipsuses.

"In many ways, whatever Spehari we meet will be a greater threat to me than Storm. Storm can only kill me." He chuckled softly. "A Spehari might be able to call in my *father*."

———

TEER'S HOPE for undisturbed sleep vanished as his dreams solidified around him, his unconscious self now standing amidst the wreckage of the farmhouse they'd defended the previous night. He could smell the scent of a just-passed storm and sighed.

"I will learn to banish you from my head," he told the creature.

"You may not get the time," Storm replied.

The scene shifted, suggesting that the callipsus was in control of this, not Teer. The body of the younger callipsus that had broken through the wall of the house reappeared.

"Her name-concept was *morning dew in thirdmoon's light*," the one-eyed man said, stepping into Teer's vision. "She was my fifth child and had lived sixty-six of your turnings of the seasons."

Fire flared in the illusion's eye as he faced Teer.

"And you robbed us not merely of her but of her memories," Storm growled. "You escaped us this time. I will admit we underestimated the El-Spehari."

A dangerous and false smile exposed teeth that shouldn't have been in any human mouth.

"Two of my children have met you and died, Teer of the Merik," the callipsus told him. "You have earned my respect, I suppose. I will consume you and absorb your memories to show it. For now, though, let us experiment with this place."

Teer felt the temperature begin to rise and realized that allowing Storm to control his dreams was dangerous. The callipsus chuckled, an alien sound that didn't belong in its avatar's human throat, and gestured fire into being around the young Merik.

It flickered along his skin and he found himself frozen, unable to move as he *felt* his skin begin to burn away from him.

Growling, he summoned his will and the colors he associated with Kard's mental magic. If he could drive back the power of the last Lord Colonel of the Sunset Brigades, he could control his own Pillars-damned dreams!

For a few more heartbeats, the fire continued to burn into his skin. Somehow, he held his focus and centered an image of Kard's magic scattering away from him. Then, instantly, the fire was gone. His skin was undamaged, like it had never happened.

Teer swallowed hard and raised his hand. In the waking world, he had speed and strength for his magic. Here, though...this was *his* dream.

He knew what Kard's magic looked like to his eyes, and he called it to him. The fire that had gathered around him reshaped itself to form a ball of heat around his hand as he turned his gaze on Storm.

"I think…" he murmured. "I think that 'experiment' sounds fascinating."

He hurled the flame at the callipsus's avatar—and for all that it was the *point*, he felt a moment of disappointment as Storm vanished before the flame hit.

Teer was alone in the wrecked farmhouse. He held onto the dream long enough to change it to the open prairie of the cattle ranch and then released it.

Rest would be hard enough after Storm's visit *without* trying to control his dreams.

12

*D*espite Storm's threats, Teer and Kard made it safely to Shellsvan. On the third night of their journey, Teer's dreams were even uninterrupted. He wasn't certain that he'd particularly scared the callipsus, but he'd at least pushed it out of his dreams for now.

They were still well short of the frontier town when Kard held up a hand. Teer pulled his mare up beside the other man and followed his pointed hand.

"Shellsvan," Kard said, unnecessarily.

They were still quite distant and it wasn't much of a town, but the cluster of buildings was also clearly more than a farm compound. A multistory tower rose in the center, probably holding a clock—though it appeared to be built of wood rather than the stone of the similar structure in Alvid.

And where Alvid was large enough to have clear subdistricts, Shellsvan didn't seem to. The only two-story buildings he could see were aligned with the tower, clearly forming a single main street. Houses were scattered around that main path, few of them large or built to any kind of grid.

The Spehari might *rule* Shellsvan but they definitely hadn't *shaped*

Shellsvan, Teer guessed. The lightly anchored sprawl was more of a Zeeanan style of settlement, from what he knew, than what the Spehari-ruled Merik built in most of the Unity.

"We are not alone," Kard warned.

Teer paused for a moment. He hadn't heard or seen *anyone*.

"I don't..."

"You have the eyes of a dragon, Teer, but not those of a soldier," Kard told him. "Look *down*."

Teer wasn't entirely sure what he was doing, but he followed Kard's instructions. He traced the lay of the land from where their horses stood across the couple of miles of open ground toward the town.

Knowing there was something there, he still spotted the trenches around the town first. The diggers had done a good job of keeping the soil intact and lifting it up to create a crude but effective illusion of intact ground from a distance, but it fell apart under examination.

A network of carefully dug trenches encircled the entire town, he judged, at least two layers deep. The whole point of them, of course, was that he couldn't tell if there was anyone in them—but there was no purpose to them at all if they were completely empty.

Still closer, though, was the dugout Kard had spotted. It took Teer studying the more-distant trenches for a few moments and then looking down closer to them again to finally spot it. What he'd taken for one of the ever-present small hillocks scattered across the broad prairies was no such thing.

It might have *started* as a natural rise, but soldiers had excavated part of it and reinforced it, creating a covered position where they could watch the approach from the east.

"I see it now," Teer murmured. He focused his attention on the dugout and smiled. "I hear them, too, though the dirt helps muffle that."

When he was paying attention, he could hear people *breathe* at a hundred paces. To have come this close without hearing anything was unusual for him.

"Keep your hands where they can see them," Kard instructed. "And follow me."

The El-Spehari kneed Clack forward, keeping his hands away from reins and weapons alike as he edged toward the dugout.

"Hullo!" he shouted out. "I'm *guessing* the trenchworks mean that the troops the locals called for are here? We're Hunters working the Eastern Territories, and we've news for your commander."

There was no response for a few heartbeats, and then a pair of women in gray uniforms emerged from the dugout, long repeaters in their hands as they studied Teer and Kard.

"Shellsvan and the area're bein' evacuated," the taller Merik woman told them, tucking a broad-rimmed gray hat over her dark hair. Her companion stopped at the edge of the dugout, with her gun visibly in her hands and only barely not pointed at Kard.

"All civilians are to proceed along the roads west to the wardtown of Reedoh," she continued. "I don' think you've business with the Captain-Magistrate or t' Major."

Teer wasn't entirely familiar with the rank structure of the Unity Army. He'd heard of "Magistrates" before, though. Those were the Spehari and El-Spehari who served as the Unity's authority and judges out along the frontier.

Among other things, they handled the wardstones—and the judicial human sacrifices that powered the magical defenses.

"Teer," Kard called back. "Show them the head."

Both women still had their hands on their guns—and Teer, at least, could tell there were two more people in the dugout with repeaters trained through concealed slits. The trench-diggers knew their job.

He kept his hands clearly visible as he pulled the sack up and opened it. Holding it to show the callipsus head without letting the "trophy" fall to the dirt wasn't easy, but it clearly served the purpose, as both of the visible soldiers recoiled.

"I understand there's a bounty on callipsuses," Kard said dryly. "We're Hunters and we had a, uh, disagreement with this one. If there's a Captain-Magistrate in town, he seems the perfect person to report in to. And to prod for our money."

The soldier chuckled mirthlessly.

"Good luck with that. *She* is as hard a blade as t' Unity commands." She shrugged and gestured her companion back into the dugout.

"But you're right, Hunter, that t' Captain-Magistrate'll want to see that. I'm afraid I don't have a horse, so you'll have to follow slow-foot me." She smiled thinly. "Try to get farther *without* me and you'll get shot."

"I was a soldier once, Sergeant," Kard replied. "There's a reason we said hello."

She eyed Kard and Teer sharply.

"Hunters riding this far out, and you old enough to have fought in the war," she observed. "I ain't gonna ask which *side* you fought on, old man. But I suggest that if you rode for Sunset, you keep *real* quiet about that with t' Magistrate.

"Taran has no love for the rebels. But that callipsus head… That'll buy you some peace, no matter what."

"Whoever I fought for, that war is long over," Kard replied, though Teer could tell something was bothering him. "Right now, there's a bunch of brain-eating monsters on the edge of the Unity. I imagine the Magistrate is more concerned about *that* than old grudges."

———

The Unity Sergeant's name was Keel. She led them on a winding path through the defenses, a confusing maze that Teer figured was meant to keep anyone from reaching the town without knowing the way.

If he'd tried to get to Shellsvan without Sergeant Keel, he was afraid he'd have hurt the horses. And that was assuming he'd seen all of the pit traps.

Teer wasn't sure that any of it would slow down, let alone *stop*, Storm and his kin. On the other hand, the callipsuses were big enough and fast enough that dropping a leg into a pit would be no better for them than for a horse.

He just figured that the big lizards could jump over the trenches. Of course, as they reached the main street, they found themselves facing down the barrels of a pair of standard ten-pound field guns.

Storm and his kin had proven difficult to kill, but Teer hoped that the *cannons* could actually hurt the callipsuses.

Past the cannons, Keel led them to what appeared to have been the main hotel in the settlement. Open-sided tents had been set up to cover rows of tables set up along the main street, and at least a hundred soldiers were currently eating.

It was funny. Teer could feel enough of Kard's emotions through their magical bond to make reading the other man relatively easy. The presence of the soldiers was both agitating the El-Spehari—and calming him.

The Unity troops were a potential danger, but they were clearly a danger that Kard knew how to handle. The older Hunter knew how to handle himself around soldiers.

Teer wasn't so comfortable being surrounded by dozens—*hundreds*—of armed Unity soldiers. He wasn't entirely sure how large the force entrenched in Shellsvan was, but there were more soldiers than he'd seen in his entire life.

And while his father might have been a Unity soldier, Teer was well aware that he was bound to the service of a man whose very existence was against Unity law. He had other reasons to dislike the Unity, but it was his service to Kard that made this dangerous.

There was something else, too. An underlayer of tension to his boss's motions that Teer didn't think was related to the soldiers. Something to do with the name Sergeant Keel had used for her commander —*Taran*.

"This way," Keel told them. "Tie your horses up at the hitching post there. T' Captain-Magistrate won't be waiting for you, but she's a busy woman!"

———

Teer had rarely seen Spehari in person and never from close up. That was part of why he'd mistaken Kard for a full-blooded Spehari when they'd first met. At the time, though, he hadn't even fully understood that the halfblood El-Spehari *existed*.

As he entered the hotel bar in Shellsvan, though, he *did* know that the El-Spehari existed. He'd been under the impression that they were almost all *dead*, but he at least knew they existed.

His initial impulse was still to class the tall, pale, woman with the knifelike ears as a full-blood Spehari. It was only with Kard in his sight, comparing the two, that Teer swiftly realized the truth: Taran was also El-Spehari.

"Captain-Magistrate, sah!" Sergeant Keel barked, snapping to attention. "A pair of Hunters entered the perimeter requesting to speak wit' you, sah!"

"And why exactly did you thin—"

"Peace, Siyans," Taran interrupted the Zeeanan officer who'd started speaking. Both Taran and her companion were paler than the Merik around them, though there were other Zeeanans in the camp.

"I presume the good Sergeant had good reason to lead two strangers into our command center," Taran continued. Her tone was gentle, but something in it told Teer that Keel was going to be in *immense* trouble if the Captain-Magistrate was wrong.

"Approach, Hunters," Taran ordered.

Teer followed Kard forward, the bag with the callipsus head suddenly heavy in his hands. He'd grown used to his boss, the bond making the El-Spehari easy to adjust to.

He had no such bond with Taran—and *she* was making no attempt to mute her presence or power. She almost *glowed* with a sense of power and life. Everything from her skin to her hair to her eyes gleamed. Even wearing a drab gray uniform with her hair cropped short in a frontier rider's rough cut, she was one of the most stunning women he'd ever seen.

"I am Captain-Magistrate Taran," she introduced herself, then indicated the Zeeanan. "This is Major Siyans, commander of the Seventy-Third Light Cavalry. These are his troops, seconded to my command alongside the Twenty-Fifth Horse Artillery."

Kard bowed and Teer tried to follow suit. Even with Kard clearly— to Teer, at least—roughening up his bow, Teer was nowhere near as graceful.

"I am Kard and this is my apprentice, Teer," the El-Spehari introduced them. "We are accredited Hunters of the Unity, and we are here to provide intelligence and claim a bounty."

Taran's soft smile wielded a power Teer wasn't sure he understood —but it shut Major Siyans up before he said a word.

"I am a Captain-Magistrate of the Unity, Hunter Kard," she observed. "I am still presuming on your sense, but it is rare that *I* am tasked with managing bounties. We leave that to the Wardwatches, not even the regular Magistrates."

"Not this bounty, my lady," Kard told her. "Teer."

Teer didn't need further instruction. He stepped up to the table Taran and Siyans were sitting at and dropped his burden on it, unsealing the bag after it landed to let it fall open and reveal their prize.

He was careful enough to make sure that no…debris…landed on the table or the papers the two Unity officers had been reviewing. But *morning dew in thirdmoon's light*'s head was very clearly visible to everyone in the hotel's front room.

"That is…very large," Siyans murmured. "I did not think they were quite so large."

"Then you have not been paying attention," Taran replied. Something in her tone told Teer that was no surprise to the El-Spehari woman. She studied the callipsus head like she'd seen them before, looking for clear markers.

"It's real," she concluded. "Fully grown but with multiple regular repeater-round exit wounds. I didn't think those could breach callipsus hide."

"We have a small number of bullets we acquired from a Kota trader," Kard admitted. "Not enough to share or sell but enough to drive them off when they came for us."

"Well, it seems these things are not as formidable as you feared, Magistrate," Siyans observed. "I suppose we can pay these fine Hunters and consider the *other* problem we have been speaking of?"

"'Them,'" Taran echoed back at Kard. "How many?"

"A breeding pair and at least two spawn," Teer's boss replied instantly. "The Kota we met said they'd killed one. We took down this one when they ambushed us at a farm they'd already massacred.

"At least two remain—and given how many dead folk there seem to be around here, I suspected they have at least one egg even if they have no older spawn left."

Siyans looked irritated at Kard's referring to the Kota.

"So, we're to rely on the lies of traveling Kota poultice salesfolk?" he asked.

"Given that this particular sales-Kota appears to have sold our friends *working* poultices, yes," Taran replied, her tone still perfectly calm. "I will need to consult my books, Hunter Kard, to see what you are owed. But you have my word, on the Midnight Proclamation and the King in Winter, that you will be paid."

No one else in the hotel bar could see through Kard's illusion—Teer hoped!—so no one else could have seen the shiver that ran through his master at the other El-Spehari's words.

This El-Spehari was, if he understood Kard's description of the Proclamation correctly, magically bound to the King in Winter with an even more powerful version of the bond that linked Teer and Kard.

The same law demanded that Kard submit to the same or die.

"For now, I grant you the hospitality of the Unity," she continued. "Eat, drink. I need some time to consider this."

She held up a hand as Teer reached for the bag.

"Leave the head, Hunter," she instructed. "I need to study it some more…and then it will need to be destroyed. The callipsuses have ways of using the minds of their fallen."

13

"Don't ask. Not here."

Teer hadn't even been thinking about asking while in a town under direct Unity control. There was no chance they could safely talk about anything while staying in the hotel hosting the cavalry forces commanders.

So far, everyone he'd seen, from the officers to the guards to the cooks and the handful of people bringing food to the officers, had worn the gray uniform of the Unity Army. Teer wasn't nearly as good at counting people as he was at counting cattle, but he was certain there were *hundreds* of men and woman scattered through the town.

He'd recognized Merik, Zeeanan and Rolin soldiers, plus at least two ethnicities he *didn't* know off the top of his head. Officially, the Unity ruled eight races including the Spehari themselves—and that number did not include the Kota, the Leeyon, the Qwah or the Kott, tribes and nations still outside the borders of the Unity. All four of those peoples were present inside the Unity, but the Spehari did not claim their nations as *part* of the Unity.

"Fair. What next?" Teer finally asked Kard. The two of them had been assigned an empty room that had probably served as a storeroom or something when the hotel was in civilian hands. There were no beds, but there was enough space for both of their bedrolls.

"We await the Captain-Magistrate's commands," his boss replied, clearly thinking his words through carefully. "She will want our full report on the encounter at the farm, but clearly she believes she can learn something from the head itself."

"Can she?"

The El-Spehari shrugged.

"I don't know," he admitted. "I've run into callipsuses before, but I have the distinct impression that Taran may be the Unity's *specialist* on the matter. She certainly was able to judge quite a bit just from the head.

"What she comes up with will likely be an education for us," Kard concluded. "Either way, we aren't moving on until the callipsuses are dead."

"Would Taran *let* us?" Teer asked.

"I don't know," Kard repeated. "In her place, with two Hunters at hand who have demonstrated they can kill a callipsus? I'd hang on to us.

"Siyans seems competent enough, but he clearly underestimates his enemy."

"He wants to chase the Kota," Teer guessed.

"Almost certainly." His boss shook his head. "And we won't give him enough of a trail for him to do anything of use with it. I won't repay them like that."

Kard clearly figured they were being overheard, Teer noted. Even in private, discretion was necessary when they were surrounded by Unity troops.

Today, the gray uniforms around them were not the enemy. But that wasn't guaranteed to last.

———

IT WAS morning by the time they were summoned back to the presence of the Captain-Magistrate. An attractive young Zeeanan soldier knocked on their door to bring them back to the main bar, her tone firm but polite.

The bar was emptier than it had been when they arrived, many of the officers present the prior day clearly elsewhere. Taran was far from alone in the room, but she'd settled herself into a back corner behind a table acting as a desk.

"Have you eaten?" she asked Teer and Kard without preamble. "No? Thought not. Kye, get them food."

The soldier saluted and vanished toward the kitchen as Taran gestured them to seats across from her. Once they had sat, she pushed a large leather pouch across the table.

"The official bounty on a callipsus is a hundred stones," she said calmly. "You may count it if you wish."

"I see only one Magistrate around here I could appeal to if the count is wrong, so I believe I shall trust you," Kard replied, sliding the pouch into his jacket while Teer tried not to choke on the number.

That was half of the annual cash sales of his stepfather's ranch, a sum that even Hardin would rarely hold in cash—and if he ever did, it almost certainly would only be for a few tendays at most before a large amount of the stamped crystals were consumed by an operating ranch's unending hunger for funds.

"Thank you, Captain-Magistrate. I believe that concludes our business?"

Kard clearly didn't believe any such thing, leaning back in his chair and glancing over to where Kye, the young soldier, was balancing three platters of food with a grim expression on her face.

"Hardly, Hunter. But please, eat with me," Taran instructed. "I need you to tell me everything you found on the eastern farms and of your encounter with the callipsus, and I know our enemy well enough to not want to hear that while eating!"

———

TARAN WAS WELL spoken and clearly well educated. She was also trying to put the two Hunters at their ease, even as she found the right questions to worm details from them that Teer hadn't meant to give away.

Kard's own careful interjections guided the conversation away from Teer's missteps. Teer followed his master's guide, listening at the careful dance of words as he realized how utterly out of his depth he was in the conversation taking place.

By the time they'd finished going over the events at the farm, Teer had a new respect for his master's ability to guide a conversation—and a sinking feeling that Taran knew they were hiding something.

"Unfortunately, my troops have found similar scenes at other farms," she told them. "There are not many as large as that one out here, but we are still looking at hundreds of deaths.

"Given that a callipsus pair only need to consume about two dozen minds between them to spawn, those numbers terrify me," the El-Spehari admitted. "This is not a few dozen deaths over the course of a turning, or a single farm wiped out in a night by a pair without patience.

"This is a planned campaign of hundreds of murders over a single turning of the seasons. I am not even certain I have heard of every death, but what I *know* of speaks to at least a dozen eggs laid."

Teer would freely admit he was bad at numbers. He hadn't followed through the logic—and from Kard's expression, his boss had been trying *not* to.

"But a callipsus can only lay an egg once every three or four seasons," the older Hunter said grimly. "So, for this slaughter to have been worth it, there has to have been more than two. Or this has been a mindless atrocity."

"My understanding of their biology suggests that is not as hard a limit as previous assessments have suggested," Taran said. She gestured, using her magic to clear the dishes and platters away.

"Kye, the map," she ordered.

The same dark-eyed Zeeanan soldier appeared. The speed with which the woman—only a turning or two past Teer's own age, he judged—had arrived with the maps suggested prior planning.

"Preexisting survey maps of the region are unimpressive," Taran noted. "Fortunately, my superiors saw fit to assign me an artillery battalion. While the Twenty-Fifth Artillery is shorter of guns than I would like, the logic of the Unity means that I still have all one hundred *gunners*.

"I've been using them as surveyors, and this map is probably the most accurate to ever exist of the area around Shellsvan."

Teer could read maps. At least to the extent of finding a town and working out which direction to go to get to it, anyway. The type of map that Kye had laid out on the table was new to him, with all kinds of extra lines and markings he wasn't familiar with.

Kard obviously was, and Teer *saw* Taran take note of that.

"We are here, at Shellsvan," she said, pointing at a large black marker on the map. "You encountered them here, two days' ride and forty-five miles away."

She pointed to a new marker, a small triangle circled in red. As Teer looked across the map, he saw the same symbol repeated. Some of the triangles were circled in blue, but there was a lot of red.

"We knew of sixty-eight farms between Shellsvan and the unofficial border at the Venedor Hills," Taran noted. "Total population was around seven hundred. The red-circled farms we know to have been massacred, from reports or our own scouts. The blue ones we have successfully evacuated, moving the populace back west toward the dragon line at Corrigan.

"Not all of that was voluntary," she said grimly, "but we have moved around four hundred from the farms and another thousand from Shellsvan itself. The only people that *should* be left in this region are my troops."

And the Sondar Tribe camp, though Teer hoped Tyrus had moved them north by now. Taran didn't know about them—not in detail, at least.

"Now." The El-Spehari studied the map, letting the word hang in the air. "You said there was an even larger callipsus with only one eye?"

"Yes," Teer confirmed. He couldn't tell the Captain-Magistrate that he knew Storm's *name*.

"Left or right?"

Teer blinked in surprise. He hadn't expected that question—and he honestly didn't know which eye Storm's real body was missing. He *did*, however, know which eye the Merik-esque avatar the being had worn in his dream had.

"Missing the left, I think," he said slowly.

"Fucker."

There was an awkward silence, then Kye returned with a tray of steaming mugs of tea. To Teer's mild surprise, the soldier took a seat next to the Captain-Magistrate. She was waiting attentively for orders, but now that Teer had a better sense of balance, he suspected there was something *more* to the young Zeeanan soldier's attentiveness.

Taran nodded her thanks to Kye and swallowed a gulp of tea that *had* to be too hot before saying anything more.

"The scent of air after the storm," she said softly. "That's what the monster called itself when I met him last, and I *thought* I'd killed the bastard."

"I didn't think callipsuses spoke," Kard noted carefully.

"They have ways," Taran replied. "And this bastard is the oldest and smartest of them I've ever met. I've hunted thirteen of the monsters in the last twenty turnings, but *this* one I met after he'd killed and eaten a Spehari Magistrate."

Kye clearly already knew about that—which added to the suggestion that she was more than the soldier who'd happened to be available—but both Teer and Kard were taken aback.

"I wouldn't have thought the Unity would let that stand," Kard finally said.

"We didn't. Three Proclamation-bound El-Spehari and three Spehari went after the bastard." Taran shrugged. "He toyed with us for a tenday before we thought we'd trapped and finished him. It appears he decided we would be easier to deceive than defeat.

"I'd like to say *I* took his eye, but the bastard was already missing that when we met him."

She glared at the map.

"You two are the only other people in this region who have faced a callipsus and lived," she told them. "I've evacuated every civilian we can find, and that order applies to you. Between that and your bounty already eating a large chunk of my discretionary fund, I won't blame you if you follow the order and head to Corrigan to grab the dragon line to safer climes.

"But...well..." Taran smiled thinly. "You *killed* a callipsus. You tell me you have bullets that can do it again. I'd be *delighted* to hire you under the Magistrate's Seal."

The Seal was how Magistrates assembled forces to deal with threats. Hunters operated with a certain degree of impunity with regards to normal laws, but they were still subject to the regular authority of Wardkeeper, Wardwatch and Mayor.

Magistrates, the Spehari who ruled the frontier, were not. And the agents they engaged under their Seal were, for the duration of their task, equally immune to Unity law.

If Kard had accepted the Midnight Proclamation and been a member of the ruling caste, Teer's bond to him would have made him equally immune. But as Kard remained the *target* of the Proclamation and not one of its servants, Teer and Kard were at risk in the Unity.

Taran's Seal wouldn't protect them from *that* particular crime, but it would put them above most attention and notice—and give them a chance to fight the war that had already overrun hundreds of innocents.

"What would you need us to do?" Kard asked, not even looking at Teer. The El-Spehari knew that Teer would at least want to listen.

"I would *like* you to talk sense into Major Siyans and get him to realize the magnitude of the danger we face," Taran admitted. "But since I can only admit that because you aren't his troops, I don't think that's likely to help."

The presence of Kye, who *was* one of Siyans's troops, went unmentioned.

"My impression, Hunter Kard, is that you were a soldier and are familiar with artillery and trenchworks?"

"I was."

Kard's bland admission was probably dangerous, Teer knew. He didn't know how unpleasant the Midnight Proclamation's effects were on the El-Spehari who'd conceded to it, but he doubted that Taran *liked* her kin who'd rebelled against the King in Winter.

"Since you have that experience and have seen how callipsuses attack, I'd like you to survey our defenses and give me your opinion," Taran told him. "I assume your apprentice goes with you?"

"Unless you need him for something else," Kard said. "He is quite capable in his own right."

Faint praise, but Teer knew that Kard meant it. Taran studied the older Hunter for a moment, then nodded in a way that suggested *she* got it too.

"In that case, I *can* use you," she told Teer. "I trust our cavalry, but an extra set of eyes who know what to look for won't go amiss. If nothing else, the more eyes in a patrol, the more likely *someone* will spot the error in the monsters' illusions."

14

Kye gave Teer a few minutes to gear up and then led him out toward the edge of town. The Zeeanan soldier was quiet, restricting herself to instructions of a few words, as she led the young Hunter to a solid-looking stable.

"Sergeant Tavis should have your horse," she told him. "Collect her and we'll find the patrol."

Star was eager to see him, as usual—and after the last few tendays, the mare seemed delighted to be only loaded down with Teer's weapons and supplies for a single day.

Well, three days. The patrol was *supposed* to be out and back again, but Teer had been a ranch hand for half a dozen turnings. *No* ride into the wilderness ever went entirely as planned.

Kye looked a bit askance at the sheer array of gear that Star carried as Teer led the mare out of the stables. He was already carrying the Kott-steel saber and his two quickshooters, which meant that his horse was now carrying both of his long guns.

"What is it you hunt, again?" she asked.

"People," Teer said quietly. "Bad people, I hope. Callipsuses count."

"I don't think I've heard even Taran call them 'people,'" Kye said.

"I didn't say they were *nice* people or *civilized* people," he told her.

85

"They're murderous people-eating monsters, Kye, but they're intelligent, magically powerful and dangerous.

"They're monsters. But they *are* people."

"That's a broad definition of *people* you're using," she pointed out.

"Well, it's a definition that includes you, me, Taran...even the Spehari and the Kott," Teer replied. "It serves a purpose."

"And being people doesn't stop them from being monsters," she conceded.

"In my experience, sadly, being a person is a requirement for being a monster."

―――――

THE PATROL they were supposed to join looked like they'd been halfway out of town when the message had caught up. Teer hung about half a horse-length behind Kye as the Unity soldier rode up to the patrol's leader.

"Sergeant Avitus," she greeted the broad-shouldered Rolin man with the shaved head. "You received your updated orders, I hope?"

"Two extras to slow us down," Avitus replied in a deep rumble, rubbing a pair of fingers over a heavy piercing in his left eyebrow. "At least I knows you. Who's this one?"

"Teer is an Accredited Hunter of the Unity, riding under Captain-Magistrate Taran's Seal," Kye said briskly. "He's also killed a callipsus, which puts him ahead of everyone in this Court-judged regiment except the Captain-Magistrate."

"Huh." Avitus turned on his horse to study Teer. A season earlier, his flat regard might have bothered Teer. Now he just returned it, keeping his opinion of the Unity troops around him buried.

None of these soldiers had any idea what they were facing. Teer and Kard, with all of their gifts and the advantage of warning, had killed *one* callipsus of three—and Teer figured that Storm could still have taken them if the old monster hadn't been thrown by the loss of his child.

"This true?" Avitus asked, now ignoring Kye. "I'm stills not convinced the beasts are even real."

"They're real enough, Sergeant," Teer replied. "And they'll eat your brain if you give 'em a chance. They'll trick you and they'll blind you and they will kill every one of your soldiers and eat them while they still breathe.

"Don't call 'em beasts, Sergeant. These 'beasts' are smarter'n you. Smarter'n me."

"Certainly smarter than the *aide*," someone muttered. "Only ting *she* knows is what's 'tween the Magistrate's legs."

Avitus was considering Teer's words. He either hadn't *heard* his trooper or he was pretending not to—but Teer didn't need to even *look* at Kye to know that the Captain-Magistrate's aide had heard the insult.

He kneed Star into motion, leaving the surprised Sergeant behind as he rode down the line of cavalry and stopped in front of the man who'd spoken. The Merik shared his Sergeant's affectation of a shaved head, though he lacked Avitus's piercings.

"You have something to say 'bout the Captain-Magistrate, Soldier?" Teer asked dryly. "It seems I'm in her service, so say your words and I'll pass 'em on to her."

The trooper clearly hadn't been expecting *that* response, and even his Merik-dark skin paled under Teer's calm regard.

"I said nothings," he finally said.

"Did you, then?" Teer told him. "Good."

He didn't give two biters' wings for the Captain-Magistrate, if he was being honest. Magistrate's Seal or not, Taran was a threat to his boss. Right now, though, they were working together to fight the callipsuses—and Teer didn't have it in him to half-do a job or let bullying go unanswered.

Giving the soldier a firm warning nod, he brought Star back up to where Avitus and Kye were waiting. The Captain-Magistrate's aide said nothing, but she looked significantly less stormy than she had before.

"I thought there was a reason for these patrols, yes?" Teer asked. "We've already delayed you, Sergeant Avitus. I feel we should get movin'."

———

"Avitus! A word?"

The woman shouting after the patrol and riding toward them was potentially the most gaudily dressed person Teer had seen in the town turned army camp. It was barely possible to tell that her uniform was supposed to be the same gray garment worn by the cavalry troopers around Teer. Her clothing was cut from a completely different and noticeably shinier fabric—and then marked in a dozen places with braid that appeared to be actual silver.

"Captain." The Sergeant turned his horse toward the woman and saluted.

"Has Sergeant Palan returned that you are aware of?" the gaudy officer asked. "She was supposed to report in about half a candlemark ago. If she's done something off-protocol…"

"I haven't seen her, sir!" Avitus replied crisply. Everything he did around the stranger was accompanied by a level of crisp precision Teer hadn't seen from the solder before.

The cavalry troopers had similarly acquired suddenly straighter backs. The entire twenty-soldier patrol had changed their entire body language when they'd realized the Captain was approaching.

"All right," the Captain groused, pausing to clearly assess the troop —exactly as her soldiers had been anticipating, Teer judged. Her gaze lingered on Teer and Kye for a moment, and he saw her lip curl at his lack of uniform.

She must have been informed of the addition to the patrol, however, as she said nothing to them and returned her attention to Avitus.

"Watch for Palan and her patrol," she ordered. "She should know better than to be late."

"As you order, Captain."

"And have your troops double-clean their saddles when you return," the Captain barked. "Their equipment is well short of the standard we expect from the Unity's finest!"

Teer glanced at the soldiers around him, making sure he wasn't completely crazy. Every piece of saddle and tack the patrol had was far cleaner than he'd expect from a troop on constant duty. It was certainly cleaner than any ranch hand he'd ever seen had managed!

"As you order, Captain," Avitus repeated, his tone submissive. "With your permission, we will commence our patrol?"

"Very well, Avitus, but make certain your troop is up to standards tomorrow! If I am embarrassed in front of the Major, we will have *words*."

Avitus bowed his head in acknowledgement and then wordlessly gestured the troop back into motion. Teer eyed the Captain for a few moments as they rode away, then put his focus on the task in front of him.

"Missing patrols?" he asked Avitus. "That's…worrying."

"Mights be," Avitus conceded. "Mights not be. Half a candlemark is nothing. Captain Rane is quite insistent on the standards of her company. We wills watch for Palan."

More to warn Palan about the *Captain* than the callipsuses, Teer judged. He didn't understand how the Unity Army worked.

He supposed he didn't need to. Today, at least, they were on the same side.

15

They rode away from Shellsvan for about a candlemark, with no sign of any other patrols or any life at all. Teer thought he spotted some deer in the distance at one point, but the prairie was shockingly empty of even wildlife.

"This whole place stinks," Avitus finally declared, pulling up his horse. "Mights not be supposed to be people, but there should be *something*."

"Captain-Magistrate says that's rare but happens with breeding pairs of callipsuses," Kye replied. "Something about them sends everything into hiding."

Teer listened hard, but all he could hear was the creak of leather tack and the breathing of the horses and soldiers around him. Not even birdsong broke the strange silence.

"We needs a wider sweep. We should have met Palan on the way out," Avitus said. "Corporals!"

His bellow drew three women, all looking a touch more hard-bitten than the rest of the patrol, now that Teer was looking at them.

"We splits by wings," Avitus ordered them as they gathered around them. "Maintain eyesight of the next wing." He gestured at Kye and Teer. "Extra weight rides with me. Meet up at Rylo's Stead."

There was none of the rigid formality the cavalry troop had shown when their Captain had ridden by. The three Corporals didn't even audibly reply to Avitus, but they split off to collect the other four riders of their wings and divide the patrol.

"They knows their places in the spread," Avitus told Teer before the Hunter could say a word. "We trains for this."

"They're better soldiers than they are tack cleaners," Kye added. "And they're damn good tack cleaners."

The Sergeant failed to swallow his snort of amusement at the younger soldier's commentary.

"'Tisn't my place to argue the Captain."

"Nor mine," Kye agreed. "It's *my* place to be the Captain-Magistrate's eyes and ears, though. There are supposed to be gains for that."

"If you says so," Avitus said, not quite dismissively. "Come on. Captain's standard or not, I won't fall behinds the other wings!"

Teer didn't say anything, just touching his heels to Star's flanks and urging her along with the Sergeant. The eerie silence of the plains soon swallowed any further conversation, the smaller seven-rider group feeling even smaller against the immensity of northern Aran.

But somewhere out there was the enemy...an enemy, who Teer had to remember, regarded *them* as *prey*.

———

OVER THE NEXT TWO CANDLEMARKS, the spread-out cavalry troop definitely covered more terrain, but even Teer didn't see anything different. The rolling prairies stretched out, their seeming consistency hiding a vast array of hills and hollows in his experience.

"Rylo's Stead is there," Avitus told him, pointing.

Teer followed the Sergeant's gesture and considered the smudge on the horizon. He focused and the structures became clearer, but they were still far enough away that he was surprised at the cavalryman's vision.

"Anything special about the farm?" he asked.

"We evacuated Rylo and their family a tenday ago," Avitus replied.

"Their herds wents with them, along with everything they could fits in wagons or tie on to the calmer cattle. Now…" A massive shrug. "Half-day's ride makes it a good landmark. Nothing special about the place, really; it's just handy. We turns most of the patrols there."

Teer nodded thoughtfully. Something about that felt…off, but he wasn't sure. And he certainly wasn't the person in charge of running patrols across a lifeless chunk of prairie, either!

He could see two of the three wings of troops Avitus had sent out. The third was beyond the horizon—he'd found he could make out details more clearly than just about everyone else, but the horizon was no more distant for him than anyone else.

"Sergeant!" their lead rider shouted. "Down here; I've found Palan's patrol!"

"They're a long-cursed ways from where they're supposed to be," Avitus growled. "Come on!"

The soldier gestured the patrol, extras included, into a canter toward where their point rider had found something. It was still in the direction of Rylo's Stead, Teer noted absently, though it appeared that there was a deep gully running across their path that the seeming blandness of the prairie had concealed.

Dipping into it, they swiftly lost sight of the separated patrols. The gully was deeper than Teer had realized, though shallow enough there to not endanger the horses. A broad but shallow stream burbled along the bottom, seemingly harmless for all that it had carved the gully over the turnings.

Following the stream north, he spotted their scout. The rider had stopped to let his horse drink and was looking farther up the gully toward…something.

There was a faint buzzing in Teer's ears, and he felt a strange feeling of vagueness sweep over him as he tried to follow the scout's gaze.

"There they are," Avitus declared, a growl of displeasure under his tone. "Come, let's find out what under the Pillars kept Palan out this long!"

There was nothing there. Teer forced his attention to where Avitus and the scout were looking, struggling against the feeling of being swathed in cotton and fog to *focus* on the gully.

There was nothing there. No scouting patrol. No riders. Now that Teer was pushing through the fog, he could see that the scout rider was almost frozen, blankly staring up the gully at something Teer couldn't see.

Avitus was looking at the same spot. So were Kye and the rest of the patrol, clearly seeing something that Teer couldn't.

"No," he whispered, then louder. "Stop, Sergeant! It's a trap!"

Avitus turned to glare at him.

"What are you ons about, Hunter?" he snapped. "Palan's patrol shouldn't be out here, so I'm guessing she has an injured trooper. We soldiers stick together, even if a Hunter like you doesn't get that!"

"Palan isn't there, Sergeant," Teer told the soldier. "There's nobody there. It's a callipsus illusion and it's a trap."

The patrol was still riding forward, and Teer wasn't even sure of the nature of the trap. The Sergeant shook his head dismissively at Teer, urging his horse forward in defiance of Teer's warning.

Swallowing, Teer did the only thing he could—he urged Star to a run, the horse coming up to speed with gleeful cooperativeness.

He drew his short repeater as he charged, searching the ground and gully sides for what he knew had to be there. So far as he knew, a callipsus couldn't leave an illusion behind. The monster *had* to be there —but he also doubted they were relying on the first round in their gun.

Heartbeats counted. Five passed before Star was out in front of the patrol. Twenty, and the mare was at full speed, carrying him forward as he searched for the trap.

Shouted exclamations followed him but Teer ignored them. Ten heartbeats after reaching full speed, Star passed the scout rider, the man still staring blankly at the air—and he saw the trap at last.

A web of fencing wire had been woven across the ground, about ankle-high on a horse. A horse might step over one or two of the wires, but there were a dozen—and if Teer had no idea what they were linked to, he certainly didn't want to find out!

He had no business asking Star to do what he needed her to do. She was a ranch horse, not a show horse or a warhorse. She'd adjusted to her new life, but to go from a gallop to a full halt in less than twenty paces was unfair.

Teer did it anyway, turning the horse toward the side of the gully so she could run up and out. Three heartbeats to guide Star away from the trap—and then he leapt from her back, relying on his preternatural reflexes to bring him safely to the ground in front of the wires.

Star was scrabbling up the side of the gully now, turning her forward speed into momentum up the steep-but-climbable slope. She was going to be fine. He hoped.

Twenty-one people behind him weren't going to be if he didn't do *something*. His repeater held in his right hand, he barely registered drawing one of the quickshooters with his left.

Wires weren't an easy target. They were barely visible and someone had put real effort into concealing them—but Teer didn't miss.

Not as a rule.

Not this time.

Five shots cracked out in as many heartbeats, each tearing through multiple wires and shredding the tripwire waiting for the cavalry behind him.

There was at least one shout of shock between his firing and the trap triggering—but any further exclamations were lost as a dozen explosive charges triggered. Blast-cotton had been embedded in the sides of the gully and linked to the wires. The area covered by the wire was instantly filled with fire and debris, stone and earth alike flung into the space where Sergeant Avitus's troops would have ridden a few moments later.

Instead, Teer was pelted with a few high-speed pebbles, afterthoughts of the weapon that could have wiped out the entire patrol. He winced away in pain, feeling where one of them had cut his cheek, and swept the wreckage of the gully for the next part of the trap.

"By the Magistrates of the Mountain Star and the Court of the Dead in which They judge us," someone whispered behind him. "What—"

"Watch!" Teer barked. "There is still—"

One of the cavalrymen screamed, flailing wildly at their body, trying to beat away an assailant no one else could see. Swords flashed into the air as chaos tore through the small group of Unity soldiers, and before Teer could finish his sentence, steel struck steel as two of the cavalry troopers struck at each other.

A gunshot cut through the chaos as Kye fired her repeater into the air.

"Lowers your blades!" Avitus barked, his harsh words aided by Kye firing a second shot into the sky as the two noncoms pulled their horses away from the chaos.

"The enemy is playing with your minds," Kye growled. "We were warned. *Shield your wills.*"

It was a Pillars-sized ask for the soldiers to ignore the evidence of their own eyes, but from the occasional half-concealed flinch on the part of the two noncoms, Teer realized that was exactly what Avitus and Kye were *doing*.

When the swordfight didn't stop, Avitus charged into the middle, using both his horse and his own bulk to knock both swords to the ground and shock his troopers into sense.

"Shields your wills," he barked, echoing Kye's words as he knocked a repeater from a third soldier's hands. "None of what you sees is real. We are under attack froms outside. What you sees *is* the attack, to breaks your wills. Will the Seventy-Third be founds wanting?!"

Once Teer was sure that Avitus was, somehow, keeping his troops under control, the Hunter turned his attention to *his* task. He could only search for the callipsus so much when his allies were about to kill each other, after all!

He wasn't sure what the range of a callipsus's powers were, but he figured it couldn't be *too* far—and then the sound of *more* gunfire sent a chill down his spine.

Teer looked over at Avitus, who met his gaze with a pained expression.

"*Go!*" the Sergeant bellowed.

Teer hit the gully side at a run, well aware he was revealing his abilities to at least one person who might know what they meant, and sprang up in a trio of bounds that delivered him to Star's side.

The mare hadn't gone far. She'd reached the top of the rise and stopped once she'd shed the momentum of her gallop, only going a few yards farther when spooked by the explosion.

Now she leaned into him as he mounted at a run. More gunfire came from the north and he was grimly certain he knew *exactly* what was happening—but it gave him a line for where the callipsus among them had to be!

———

THERE WASN'T a single claw mark on the wing of cavalry when Teer finally found them. All five were dead, but he didn't have very far to look for their killers. The cartridges and weapons scattered with the corpses told a clear story.

Without someone with them to realize they were under attack and warn them against the illusions, five of the Unity's soldiers had killed each other.

There was nothing Teer could do for them. He could see Avitus and his troopers struggling to get their horses over the edge of the gully behind him, and he turned his focus to the next task.

Where was the callipsus? He could feel the buzz of its power in the back of his head, but he hadn't seen any sign of the monster. Not even tracks—though Teer knew he was a barely passable tracker, relying entirely on his superior senses.

He moved away from the carnage where the troopers had fallen, urging Star through a spiraling loop as he searched for the tracks of the enemy that *had* to have come close. The illusions would affect the victims for some time once the callipsus had left, he figured. But the creature had to be present to *create* them, which meant it had started near Avitus's wing and headed north.

Thankfully, the *other* two wings were south of there. Unless the callipsus had turned around, it wasn't heading toward more of Avitus's troops.

Teer was sadly certain of what had happened to Sergeant Palan now. They might have missed the other patrol during their ride…but it seemed more likely that they had also been ambushed.

There.

For a twelve-foot-tall lizard, a callipsus was astonishingly light-footed. Still, they were large enough and heavy enough that leaving no tracks was impossible. This one was being clever, using stands of grass to try to hide their tracks.

Now that Teer had found a handful of visible prints, though, he had the trail. Dismounting, he took a few heartbeats to check the prints. The creature had come from the south, he judged, and stopped *here*, to engage and destroy the patrol.

He wasn't sure, but it looked like the callipsus had stopped for less than a hundred heartbeats. A hundred heartbeats to turn five soldiers who had served and fought together for seasons on each other.

Teer refused to call his enemy *beasts*, but *monsters* was starting to come far more easily to his mind. He could, *barely*, accept that the callipsuses were forced to eat people to have children. He wasn't going to let that *happen*, but he could at least *consider* that it might not be truly evil.

This, though. To play with brave soldiers' minds and turn them on each other?

Teer would rather take a straight fight any day. Convincing a callipsus to have one of those, he was realizing, was harder than he'd thought. He'd surprised one once, and Storm had underestimated the combination of his and Kard's power.

But now the callipsuses were coming to war. There was no way they *didn't* know what Taran had gathered in Shellsvan—which meant that the attacks on the patrols had to be part of a plan.

Even as he ran through the threat, he was following the tracks. He carried his repeater in his hands and drew a strange sense of comfort from the weight of the Kott-steel saber on his hip. He knew the quick-shooters best, but they weren't going to hurt a callipsus.

The trail wasn't getting any fresher. If anything, his enemy was getting farther ahead of him—but its head start was only a few hundred heartbeats. He should be able to *see* the creature…

It was Star's whinny that warned him, the horse trailing half a dozen feet behind him—her whinny and then the spike of pain in his head as he became the full and sole focus of the creature's power.

His eyesight failed him, sparks of color and pain overwhelming him as the callipsus hammered its will into him. It couldn't make him see what it wanted, so instead, it made him see *nothing*.

But Teer could still hear, and that gave him enough warning to sidestep, leaving the callipsus's claws to slash through where he'd stood. He could *hear* the monster move now, and he focused on the sounds, trying to judge where it was well enough to avoid being hit.

His vision was overwhelmed and pain tore through his skull, but he could still move. Just not fast enough.

His right cheek was the unlucky one. Already torn open where the debris from the explosion had hit him, it now lit up with searing fire as a claw slashed through his flesh—missing most of his face, still, and glancing off his shoulder blade.

Teer jumped blindly, leaping forward to buy himself distance. The impact shook away much of the darkness shrouding his eyes, and he realized the repeater was still in his hands—and he could *see* the callipsus now.

His sight was still a matter of shadow and shape through the pain and the light the monster was hitting him with, but he knew the shadow and shape of Star—which meant the *other* massive shadow was the callipsus.

Teer missed his first shot. The blessed bullet went wide as the pain threw off his balance and coordination, and the callipsus charged, refocusing its power.

"Fire!"

Neither Teer nor the callipsus had seen Avitus and his patrol catch up. Six repeaters fired as one, and if only half of them hit, it was still enough to throw the giant lizard off its charge. Its power flickered, and Teer could see properly at last.

Three of Tyrus's blessed bullets blazed out from his repeater in a single heartbeat as Teer strained the mechanism to its utmost while he could still see. The first tore apart the monster's hip, crippling it before it could rise. The second ripped through an eye, returning the favor of blindness—as much by mistake as anything else.

The third landed *exactly* where Teer meant, the heavy Kotaenchanted bullet smashing through the callipsus's neck and severing its spine.

It was dead after he'd finished firing. Not that Teer *stopped* Avitus and his troopers from emptying their repeaters into the monster to be sure.

16

"**Y**ou're bleeding, Hunter," Avitus told him gruffly. "Holds still."

"I've got it," Kye said, the aide producing a bag emblazoned with a blue circle. "Hold still."

Teer grimaced but nodded. Star trotted up to him, and he leaned against the horse as Kye set to work with cleansing powder on his wounds.

"Do all Hunters move like that?" she murmured to him.

"No," he confessed.

"Take off your shirt," she ordered.

"We owe you our lives, Hunter," Avitus said, stepping into the conversation as Teer obeyed. "My other two wings are catching up, but…I saw Yala's troops. The callipsus…"

"Turned 'em on—*ow*—each other," Teer agreed. Cleansing powder hurt a lot more than the Kotan poultices that had been used on his injuries in the past.

"I don't think the claw cut muscle," Kye told him. "The powder should numb you to this next bit."

Teer didn't have a chance to ask what she meant before the needle pierced the skin around the wound. If the powder *was* numbing him, he didn't want to know what getting stitched up felt without it!

"Palan's patrol is dead, aren'ts they?" Avitus asked.

"Yes," Teer said bluntly. "I fear…every patrol sent out today or last night is. They are preparing for something."

"Aye. If they's eliminating patrols, they's moving against the regiment. I just don't sees why."

"I think— *Fuck, ow!*"

"Focus on the Sergeant," Kye told him. "Do you *want* to go back to Shellsvan with your shoulder hanging open?"

That image got a bitter chuckle out of him. He was figuring they would ride back into an open battle. Nothing *good* was going to come of the callipsuses moving against Taran and Kard.

"I think it's about the eggs," he managed to finish. "They've swept this region, fed on innocents, spawned…but the eggs still need to hatch."

He hissed a breath as he finished speaking, failing to control his reaction to the pain. He felt more than a bit silly, reacting as badly to the stitching as he was.

"I didn't expects them to use explosives," Avitus said. "But evens so…they can't use wagons, cans they?"

"From what the Captain-Magistrate has said, they can't use horses," Kye said, leaning back from Teer to examine her handiwork. "Animals *hate* the smell of them. I guess they could pull the wagons themselves, but…"

Teer considered his dream conversations with Storm and shook his head.

"I think they would rather kill an entire regiment of the Unity than do that," he admitted. "They must be figuring that if they wipe out the troops in Shellsvan, they'll have time to hatch the eggs and move before more arrive."

"More *will* come," Avitus said firmly. "The Captain-Magistrate broughts a regiment and a battery. But if a Magistrate and alls her soldiers are killed? They will send *brigades*, nots regiments."

And Spehari, not El-Spehari, Teer presumed. He doubted that he'd seen the full extent of Kard's power, and his boss was generally clear that many Spehari were more powerful than him.

"But that will take time," Kye agreed. "We need to warn the Captain-Magistrate and the Major."

"Just waitings on my other wings," Avitus replied. "Then we wills ride back. If the other patrols are lost, we mays be the only warning."

"And the rest of the regiment will need the warning," Teer said. "You've faced their power and lived. You can warn the rest what that feels like."

"We will," the Sergeant said flatly. "Thanks to you, Hunter. Will he live, Kye?"

"He'll live. Even heal," she confirmed. "I'm no surgeon, but I think you will be fine if you avoid using your arm too much."

Teer chuckled bitterly.

"We shall see what the callipsuses think of that idea!"

———

RIDING HURT. Kye had done a good job of stitching Teer up, but the patrol was riding at full speed back toward Shellsvan. They had only a few candlemarks to make a trip that had taken half a day going the other way—no one wanted to ride across the prairie in the dark.

The gully they'd been ambushed in wasn't the only one of its kind, and hitting one of those in the dark could have fatal consequences.

But as Star kept up the distance-eating canter she'd rarely needed to sustain as a ranch horse, the continued bouncing pulled on his fresh stitches. Teer suspected he was going to have an ugly scar across his face. The Unity medical kit Kye had used was sufficient to heal the wound, but it wasn't the Kotan magic that had been used on his injuries in the past.

That had healed worse injuries with barely a scar. Cleansing powder and stitches would help him heal, but he suspected his face would always show the callipsus's mark.

Part of what was keeping Star going, he feared, was her distress at her new cargo: once again, the poor mare was hauling a callipsus's head toward Shellsvan. Teer hoped that Taran would be able to learn something from the dead creature—but he was also bringing it for proof of just what was happening to the cavalry patrols.

He wasn't sure how many people had been killed since sunrise, but if *every* patrol was twenty riders and theirs was the only one coming back…

Teer was no soldier. He had no idea how many patrols would have been sent out, but he figured that Storm's kin had killed at least a hundred Unity soldiers today. He wasn't certain of the strength of Major Siyans's regiment, but he guessed it somewhere between four hundred and a thousand soldiers.

Whatever Taran was planning, she'd just lost a good chunk of her troops *and* the reports she was expecting to warn her if the callipsuses were coming.

Teer was no soldier but he still figured that was a very bad thing.

Distant thunder rumbled across the prairies, and he grimaced. The last thing they needed was a storm.

The sky was clear, though. He looked around him in confusion and shivered as thunder rumbled again.

"What is it?" Kye asked. The Captain-Magistrate's aide had been riding next to him since they'd started back. He wasn't sure who she thought was protecting who, but she was also keeping an eye on his wounds.

"I hear thunder," he told her. She'd already seen enough to leave him in serious trouble with Taran, after all. "But there's no clouds in the sky."

The soldier was silent for a few long moments, her gaze suddenly focused ahead of them. Toward Shellsvan.

"Where?" she asked.

It took Teer a moment to try to sort out the direction he'd heard the thunder from—but another round made it clear. The sound was coming from ahead of them. From *Shellsvan.*

And it was far too regularly timed to be thunder.

"Shellsvan," he said grimly. "It's the guns, isn't it?"

17

By the time they came within sight of the town, Teer had become more familiar with the sound of a ten-pound rifled field gun than he ever wanted to be. He could count the separate guns firing from this distance—six. Since there were *ten* cannons in Shellsvan, he had to hope that meant the callipsuses hadn't breached the town itself.

"What are they *shooting* at?" Avitus demanded as the Sergeant stood up in his stirrups, looking across the distant town. "I sees the shell hits, but I don't sees anything *there*."

Following Avitus's gesture, Teer also spotted the impact site closest to them. It helped that a trio of shells hit the ground as the Sergeant asked his question, their explosive charges sending plumes of dirt into the air.

He hadn't known enough to recognize the impacts on his own. The second explosion of each salvo had been buried in the earth, smothering the sound and keeping him from recognizing it.

Focusing his gaze on the craters, a familiar faint buzzing sounded in his ears, and he grimaced.

"Illusions, Sergeant," he told Avitus. "The callipsuses are playing games."

"Running the guns outs of shells," the Sergeant said grimly. "Our supply train outs here is trouble. Weak. We don't have the troops to guards the wagons enough to brings shells."

Teer could only guess how many shells he'd heard fired, but it had to be well over a hundred. If the battery had limited stocks of ammunition, they could be in real trouble.

"Let's get into town and warn them," he said with a calm he didn't feel. He wasn't sure *how* they could avoid wasting shells on callipsus illusions. Even Kard and Taran couldn't pierce them reliably, after all!

So far as Teer knew, he was the *only* person in the town who could see through the monsters' magical lies.

A spike in the volume of the buzzing that turned the sound into pain was the first warning he got. He didn't realize what it was warning *of*—until the next round of shells hurtled over their heads to explode behind them, debris splattering across the rearmost riders.

"Oh, Court Judge me," one of the Merik Corporals snarled. "They're shooting at *us!*"

"Ride!" Avitus barked. "Ride like the wind, troopers—if we can stay ahead of the illusions, we can stay ahead of the shells!"

Teer wasn't sure if it worked like that…but he didn't have any *other* suggestions! He put his heels to Star's flanks, urging the already-weary horse up to a gallop and urging the mare to stay with him.

If they slipped or slowed, their own allies' shells would kill them. He put his hand on her neck, willing some of his own preternatural vitality into her. He didn't know if that would *work*, but it wasn't the craziest idea he'd ever tried!

More shells fell behind them as Avitus and the rest of the patrol bolted forward. One of the riders didn't move fast enough and didn't even have time to scream before horse and soldier alike vanished in a spray of debris and blood.

There nothing Teer could do. Even if he somehow shot the shells out of the sky, the shrapnel would still scythe through the riders. He guessed where the next shell would land, twisting Star to the left and unconsciously guiding the rest of the patrol with him.

It was enough that the shells only sprayed them with dirt this time —but the gap between that salvo and the next was too short for them to reach the trenches. He could tell that the next set of three shells was going to bracket them. There was no way to run to escape the incoming fire, and all Teer could think to do was put his head down over Star's and push her forward.

Except instead of annihilation, all the shell explosions did was batter his ears. Looking up again, he saw the debris from the shells falling all around the running patrol—and Kye holding her left arm up, palm outwards with a crystal bracelet of some kind wrapped around her fingers.

A *red* crystal bracelet, of the kind that could hold Spehari power.

"*Ride!*" she bellowed. "I don't know if this can hold another shot!"

Teer saw Avitus salute the aide as his troops charged past her, forming a moving barrier around the woman keeping them all alive.

He joined them, but the magical shield Kye was holding gave them one more chance—they weren't going to avoid the next salvo, but if the shield could stop the *shrapnel…*

His right quickshooter was in his hand before he even finished the thought, the weapon rising by instinct and training. He'd hunted game birds on the prairie, but that had been with a thunderbuss or even a hunter.

The drill was the same and his hand-eye coordination was impeccable. He had *heartbeats* to act—and emptied the quickshooter's five-round cylinder in those heartbeats.

All three shells exploded in the air, shrapnel and debris hammering into the shield from Kye's bracelet—and he heard the soldier hiss as the crystal flared hot enough to burn her skin.

Then they were in the trenches, the patrol's horses leaping the first trench at their rider's command. They careened to a halt in a chaotic mill, Teer following Avitus in sliding from his horse's back as the Sergeant charged toward the command post.

A familiar gaudily dressed woman rose from the post, shouting and corralling a squad of cavalry into a rough firing line—but Avitus reached Captain Rane first.

"Rebels!" she screamed, only to be at least momentarily silenced by the Sergeant's meaty fist.

"This is the weapons of the enemy!" Avitus bellowed. "They's in your minds! *Shields your wills!*"

The squad Rane had gathered were suddenly lost, something about both Avitus being present and him coldcocking the Captain half-breaking the illusion.

Finally able to breathe for a few seconds, Teer turned inward, pulling on his link with Kard.

He didn't know if he could *communicate* along it, but he tried. He needed his boss to know that he was inside the perimeter and under attack. Pillars, he needed Kard to know that the guns were wasting shells at *best*!

"On your left," Kye barked. "Soldiers, lower your guns!"

Teer twisted and saw the troops coming. A similar twenty-strong cavalry troop to Sergeant Avitus's was moving their way, repeaters at the ready as they trotted forward with perfect discipline.

He knew that none of the troops around him were going to shoot first. But outnumbered and facing competent enemies, the first salvo from the approaching Unity soldiers would be the end of them all.

Then *power* pulsed at the heart of town. Teer saw a ball of green light explode outward from Shellsvan, rippling across buildings and troopers with no visible effect...and yet...

As it washed over him, the buzzing at the back of his head finally broke. As it washed over the troopers around them, the lost and dazed reaction spread. Rapidly. The troop of soldiers, moving forward and expecting fire a few seconds earlier, paused in mid-maneuver, staring at people they now recognized as friends.

"What was *that*?" Teer asked.

"I don't know," Kye said. "I... What happened? A moment ago, they were going to shoot us!"

None of the others had seen it, which told Teer at least *some* of the answer. That had been Spehari magic, probably Taran's.

"Sergeant, Kye...we need to get to the Captain-Magistrate," Teer told them. "I suspect she may have just saved our lives, but she needs to *know* what we saw."

"Agreed." Avitus looked down at his superior officer and

grimaced. "Not leasts because I just punched an officer, which is a hanging crime."

"Nobody who saw what happened recognized you," Kye said instantly. "I certainly saw nothing."

"Bring your troops," Teer ordered. He wasn't entirely sure if people were going to listen, but if barking orders was what the Army expected, then he'd bark orders.

They had too much work to do to play games.

<h1 style="text-align:center">18</h1>

Somehow, Taran didn't look at all surprised to see the battered patrol ride up to the hotel. The Captain-Magistrate was out front, her pale hair and skin rendering her almost ghostlike in the setting sun.

"Sergeant Avitus. Lieutenant Kye. Hunter Teer," she greeted them. "I am pleased to see you all alive and well."

Despite her formal words and stiff body language, Teer could tell that Taran only truly had eyes for Kye. There was more truth to the accusation of Kye being the Captain-Magistrate's lover than Teer had presumed.

Not that it mattered. The bracelet Taran had given Kye had saved all of their lives.

"I am *told*," Taran continued, "that we were under attack by the sort of hastily raised rebel militia that the callipsuses have raised in the past, with pressure on the trenches only being held off by prodigious use of ammunition.

"But given the sudden silence when Hunter Kard convinced me that we were being fooled, I now fear the worst. Dismount. Report!"

"If your guns shelled anyone, it was your own patrols," Teer said flatly as he obeyed her orders. "The callipsuses have spent the day luring your patrols into ambushes and using mind magic to turn them on each other."

"When we returned, we cames under fire from the artillery in the town," Avitus said quietly, his gaze at the ground once he'd dismounted. "We lost soldiers getting through—and we would have been killed by our own people at the command post without whatever broke the illusion."

"May the Court of the Dead judge me a fool," Taran cursed herself. "I have learned many tricks fighting these monsters, Sergeant, but it requires me to *use* them. I cannot sustain a shield over the town, though I can break and scatter their powers."

Kard emerged from the hotel behind Taran, Major Siyans behind him.

"Your casualties, Sergeant?" the Captain-Magistrate asked, without paying attention to the two behind her.

"Hunter Teer was wounded by the callipsuses. Corporal Rigan and her soldiers were turned on each others by mind spells and wiped out. Troopers Bilpa and Sorch were killed by our own artillery as we tried to reach the town."

Taran nodded grimly.

"Understood, Sergeant. Take your troops into barracks. Rest and check your gear. I suspect this is not the end of their attacks tonight."

Avitus nodded and turned to gather his troops. Kye and Teer remained, waiting for further instructions.

"Hunter Kard, see to your man," Taran said.

"We have another head, if it will be of use," Teer told her.

"It may," she conceded. "Siyans!"

The Major stepped forward.

"Get someone to deal with it—and with the Hunter's and Lieutenant's horses. Both of them need rest."

Siyans looked like he wanted to say something unfortunate, but he bit down on it and nodded grimly.

"Come on," Kard told Teer. "We can trust them to take good care of Star, and I want to check your wounds."

KARD BARRED the door behind them, and Teer gave him a questioning look.

"We don't have time for you to be injured," his master told him. "Show me your wounds."

As Teer shed his damaged coat and shirt, Kard similarly shed his illusory self. Teer was still not always used to seeing his boss's true appearance, but it was necessary for Kard to unleash his magic.

The El-Spehari studied his wound for a few moments.

"Whoever treated this did a good job," he conceded. "I can't do much for your face; sorry. But we can't afford the shoulder injury slowing you down."

"Went right through the armor," Teer grumbled.

"I've heard of callipsuses slicing field guns in half," Kard said. "Hold still."

Blue light flickered around Kard's hand as he touched the carefully stitched injury. It flowed into Teer's flesh, and for a few seconds, all Teer could feel was the itch.

He managed not to move as his skin crawled back together, driven and guided by Kard's magic. The itching faded and he exhaled a long breath.

"The stitches are left," Kard told him. "The surface wound is still visible, in case someone checks, but the muscle and flesh beneath are solid now. You can move. You can fight."

"I'm going to need to, aren't I?"

"I didn't have as exciting a day as you did, but I spent it listening to the Captain-Magistrate," Kard said. "This whole town is bait, Teer. These troops, even the guns—they're too vulnerable to the callipsuses' powers.

"I've never heard of or seen anything like this. I've been part of teams that have gone after single callipsuses before, but to face an entire clan like this? I was afraid when I thought there were *two* left."

"How many do you think there are?" Teer asked, fear drying his mouth.

"Taran's math is…impeccable," Kard told him quietly. "Three hundred minimum missing or dead. For a reliable spawning, according to her, they need fifteen minds. So, twenty spawnings.

"But a mated pair can only lay one egg every three or four seasons. So each of those spawnings required a mated pair." Kard shook his head.

"Neither of us have ever heard of that many callipsuses gathered together, but Taran says that if any of them could pull it off, it would be *the scent of air after the storm*. She seems to think he's something unique."

"He's been in my head," Teer pointed out. "I don't disagree with her." He eyed his boss. "And you know her."

It wasn't a question. Kard was taking Taran's opinions and knowledge too solidly for the El-Spehari woman to be a stranger to him.

"I trained her. Thirty turnings ago. And the first time she went after a callipsus, I led the team that she was with," Kard said quietly. "She's good, Teer. And she's intentionally *not* playing guessing games."

"I don't understand."

"She is Bound to the Midnight Proclamation," the older man reminded him. "If she realizes there's an Unbound El-Spehari around, that Binding will force her to act. But so long as she only *suspects* and doesn't investigate enough to *prove*, the Bond will not compel her."

"It's a deadly balance she walks."

"One that might end up killing you both," Teer said. "And me."

He shook his head.

"It took everything I had to get that patrol back alive, Kard, and if Kye tells Taran… There aren't people like me for a reason."

"We both know that my people wiped out any magic in the Merik," Kard said. "I wish I could believe differently, but I don't. That said, Taran's Binding shouldn't have anything do with that. So, even if Kye tells her, she's likely to let it stand.

"If nothing else, you saved Kye's life and brought that patrol back alive. And I suspect both of those mean something to her."

"You got that from them too, did you?" Teer asked with a chuckle. "If they think they're keeping it under wraps, the entire *regiment* appears to think it's bullshit."

"It's a deadly balance she walks," Kard repeated. "Even if they *haven't* acted on it, enough people have recognized what's going on to cause a problem—so, regardless of whether they're sleeping together or not, Taran has to walk the line between her personal feelings and the needs of her role."

"Kye has some kind of protective charm from Taran," Teer told his boss. "It saved our lives out there, but it makes me suspect that they might not be entirely well behaved."

Before Kard could respond to that, there was a sharp rapping on the door.

"It's Kye," a familiar voice barked through it. "Are you decent?"

Teer gave Kard a panicked look, but the illusion of a tall Merik was falling back into place as the younger man pulled his shirt back on. It took them a moment to be presentable, then Kard rose and removed the bar.

The door swung open to reveal the young Zeeanan officer. Kye had clearly neither changed nor bathed since they'd parted ways, still looking sweat-slicked and worn out.

"The Captain-Magistrate wants you both," Kye told them flatly.

Teer exchanged a glance with Kard.

"We accepted her Seal," Kard said. "For the moment, we are hers to command."

———

TEER WAS surprised when Kye led them out of the hotel. His impression had been that Taran was using the building as her main command center, and he'd expected whatever meeting the Captain-Magistrate needed them for to take place there.

Instead, Kye led them down the street to a stone building that sent a shiver of familiarity down Teer's spine. Shellsvan was too small to have a wardstone or a proper Wardkeeper, but the stone building serving as the town's jail clearly was intended to act as the anchor for the type of tower that served as office for such an individual—even though the clock tower a hundred paces away was closer to that kind of structure.

Given that Teer had ended up in the jail cells of a proper Ward-watch's tower, the stone jail was enough to give him unpleasant memories. Still, he followed Kard and Kye into the structure.

The inside was different enough to calm his fears. It clearly *was* a prison, but the layout wasn't the same—and Kye was ignoring everything on the main floor, guiding them down the hall past the cells to a heavy door quite unlike anything Teer had seen in Alvid's wardtower.

Despite being large and bound in iron, with hinges armored against someone being clever, the door was perfectly balanced and swung open at Kye's touch.

Stepping through the door, the aide grabbed a portable redcrystal light from a niche in the wall and looked back at them.

"Come on, then," she told them. "The cellar of a wardtower isn't *that* scary, is it?"

"I can't say they are places I've spent much time," Kard murmured. "I didn't think there *was* a wardtower here."

"Not yet," Kye said. "But the jail is always built to support one when the time comes, isn't it?"

Teer didn't know anything about that and just shrugged. His past fears seemed surprisingly small versus the current fear—if there were thirty or more callipsuses out there, he wasn't certain that the army Taran had gathered in Shellsvan was going to be enough.

So, he followed Kye into the cellar, Kard one step behind him on the roughly shaped stairs. Stone and wood panels held back the dirt around them, suggesting looser ground than most places Teer had seen with any kind of underground structure.

It seemed stable enough as they reached the bottom of the stairs and encountered a second heavy door. This one was even larger and heavier, looking to be made more of stone and metal than wood, but was already propped open.

The door was the only thing visible from the stairs. The entire cellar was actually a vault, well secured against physical intrusion—and Teer didn't have the skills to speak to magical intrusion.

He *could*, however, see a faint green light illuminating the room on the other side of the vault door. A familiar light, one he'd seen every time he'd visited the wardtown near his home.

There were only three people in the vault waiting for them. Captain-Magistrate Taran was standing in the center of the vault, looking down at the perfectly circular gray stone in the center of the cellar.

Major Siyans and a second officer, a Merik man Teer hadn't met yet, stood around the wardstone, looking at it with the combination of fear and respect such a powerful artifact deserved.

"Why are *they* here?" the Merik man demanded.

"Because I asked them to be," Taran replied. "There are three people in this town, Captain Pan, who have killed a callipsus. Me—and these two Hunters. Our plan will rely upon them."

"Our plan will rely upon my guns."

"Assuming they shoot the enemy and not our own people," Siyans growled. "I lost too many troopers to friendly fire today. We have underestimated our enemy."

"I am glad that we finally agree upon that," the Captain-Magistrate told her subordinates. "I have an answer to that particular little problem, but the timing must be precise."

She gestured Teer, Kard and their guide forward.

"Lieutenant Kye has served as a useful sounding board for planning this," Taran observed. "It is often handy to need to explain one's thoughts to someone who is completely lacking the background. Though Kye picks up faster than most."

Teer wondered if the El-Spehari realized how much the tone of her voice was giving away—or if, amongst this collection of her closest subordinates, she even cared.

"The key to all of this is in front of us," she continued, laying her hand on the wardstone. "Shellsvan is not large enough in herself to justify a wardstone. Her position along the frontier, however, meant she'd been moved up the list. This stone was delivered under a Magistrate's guard eleven tendays ago. No one in the town knew it was here, which means that our enemy should not know it was here."

Taran looked around the room.

"Remember that the callipsuses now know *everything* their victims knew," she warned. "We will have no surprises in the layout of the town. Unfortunately, we can even be quite certain that there will be no surprises in the layout of our defenses."

"I'm surprised that the bastards know us well enough to throw imaginary rebel militia at us," Siyans admitted.

"The problem, Major, is that this particular callipsus has thrown very real rebel militia at Spehari hunting him in the past," Taran said grimly. "By means not understood by the Unity, a callipsus can give a member of any of the Arani races a fragment of their power. Those people—those *traitors*—can use that power to become extraordinarily persuasive and dangerous.

"*The scent of air after the storm* has raised armies against us before. I did not think to doubt the reality of the attack."

"And so, our own arms slew dozens of my people," Siyans said grimly. "We cannot let that happen again, Captain-Magistrate. I do not know how to fight an enemy that can turn our own guns upon us!"

"I do."

Taran's calm confidence seemed to ease her subordinates' minds, and she laid her hands on the wardstone.

"Inside a ward, no power of the mind can infect our soldiers," she explained. "More, if I empower it correctly and at the right time, the callipsuses will be trapped inside the ward. They will have no choice but to find the wardstone.

"They will have no choice but to come to me—and when they do, Captain Pan's guns will be waiting.

"Loaded with dragonshot canister."

Teer had no idea what that meant, but it was immediately clear that everybody *else* in the room did. Taran gave him a sympathetic smile.

"Canister, Hunter Teer, is a fixed cartridge loaded with regular bullets," she explained. "Stormshot canister is a fixed cartridge loaded with heavy slugs, less than half a dozen in a ten-pounder three-inch shell."

"And dragonshot fills the rest of the shell with incendiaries," Kard finished. "Let us be *very* certain we can prevent the monsters getting into our people's minds before we load those rounds, Captain-Magistrate. I saw them used in the Sunset Rebellion. I would rather not see them turned on the Unity's soldiers again."

"Aye," Captain Pan agreed. "I hesitate to even load my storm-wracked guns, Captain-Magistrate. This enemy is terrifying."

"Then you understand our foe at last," Taran said flatly. "Major Siyans, we do not know when the callipsuses will attack or what tricks or lies they will use. But your soldiers must be prepared to abandon the trenches and fall back.

"We need to lure the callipsuses, especially *the scent of air after the storm*, into the town. Once we have done so, I will charge the wardstone. *The scent of air after the storm* will be able to find it," she warned, "so they will come for the jail. And Captain Pan's guns will be ready."

"Against illusion and trickery, how are my people supposed to know when to fall back?" Siyans demanded.

Teer *felt* Taran's gaze turn to him.

"Hunter Teer," she said formally. "Lieutenant Kye tells me that you can see through callipsus illusions."

"Sometimes," he said cautiously. "It's not a reliable thing."

"I understand," Taran said. "I have known a few Merik over the turnings who are more resistant to illusions than most. It is a rare gift but a useful one. Captain Pan and his troops have erected an observation tower they use to direct fire."

"To our detriment, so far," the artillery officer grumbled. "If we can get real use of the Court-judged thing…"

"If you are willing, Hunter Teer, I would have you take a position in the observation tower with Captain Pan in the morning," Taran concluded. "From there, you will be able to see when the callipsuses start their true approach and send a signal to fall back."

"They may recognize the trap," Kard warned.

"They may," she agreed. "But they should not be aware that the wardstone exists. Without that, the trap should seem far less dangerous to them. They will likely believe that by magic and force, they can break out of whatever plan we have.

"But once the ward has been raised at full power, there will be no escape. They will be trapped inside the dome, and their illusions will be neutralized. Between the guns and my powers, we should be able to contain and annihilate a significant number of them.

"If we can destroy *the scent of air after the storm* himself, the rest of his little clan will likely scatter. We will still need to hunt down their spawning ground and destroy the eggs, but without that elder monster, they will become a more manageable threat."

Teer held his peace. From what both Kard and Taran had said, the Unity's usual approach to a callipsus was to send three Spehari after it. So far as Taran knew, they had *one* El-Spehari to face an unknown number of the monsters.

He suspected that she knew *exactly* how difficult the situation she'd walked into was going to be—and that Captain-Magistrate Taran saw no other option but to handle the fight on her own.

Everything else around the town of Shellsvan was just to trap the callipsuses on a street with her.

19

Wind whistled across the yard at Hardin's ranch house as Teer stood in the doorway. He didn't remember what he'd been dreaming a moment before, but he could somehow *tell* the moment it had stopped being an ordinary dream.

"Meet me in the open, killer of my kin," a familiar voice told him in a gently mocking tone. "I will not enter the fortress of your mind. You may think of it as having taught me respect."

Teer didn't think that ignoring Storm would allow him to return to regular sleep. He wasn't sure *how* the callipsus could insert itself into his dreams, but while he had enough control to defend himself—somehow—he didn't seem to be able to get rid of the monster.

Sighing, he stepped out of the house into the yard. One of his mother's chickens bawked at him, skittering across the packed earth—and then vanished along with the ranch. Only the open prairie and the wind remained.

And the scent of air after the storm. Both the scent itself and the being who wore it as a name.

"Why do you bother with the illusion?" Teer asked, studying the one-eyed old man. "I know what you are."

"I have less control here than you think," Storm replied, closing the distance until he stood just outside arm's reach. "Your mind shapes this. To be a *person*, in *your* unconsciousness, is to be a mutated ape of some sort."

"If you're here to taunt me, I'm not sure why we're wastin' our time," Teer said.

"*Wind over prairie streams*," Storm told him. "That was his name. Before you decided to chop off his head, that is."

"And how many cavalry troopers did he kill over the last few days? How many more died in your illusory attack that turned the artillery on their own brothers and sisters?"

Storm smirked.

"We defend ourselves, Teer. The deaths of the farm folk were an unfortunate necessity for the birth of our next generation. Just like you would not slaughter all your cattle, we did not plan to kill *everyone* here.

"But the Captain-Magistrate brought her army, and now my clan and I must defend ourselves. You understand, I know, the urge to defend one's family and friends."

"And that is why I will destroy you," Teer told the monster. "I can accept, if I must, that you must kill to breed. You have no choice—but I will still destroy you to protect *my* people."

"That is a point of view I can respect, ," Storm said grimly. "You have killed or helped kill three of my children and grandchildren, Teer of the Merik. There is a price to be paid for that."

"There is a price to be paid for the *hundreds* you slaughtered. We shall see who pays first."

The old man threw his head back and laughed.

"You remind me of her, you know. There aren't many of your kind whose minds I can touch like this," he told Teer. "Like you, Taran carries the gifts of the old Adepts. Unlike you, she also wields her father's power. Any strength from her Merik blood she has always believed to be of Spehari origin."

"She's going to kill you," Teer said conversationally.

"Captain-Magistrate Taran has come closer than most, but she won't succeed this time any more than she did last time," Storm said. "A great many people, of both the Unity and *the rising hunger of the living minds* alike, will die in the morning. I do not wish to sacrifice my children to the guns of my enemy, but a dozen may pass into memories so that two dozen can be born.

"It is a trade we knowingly make. A risk we choose so that our children may live. But you, Teer of the Merik…you can change so much of that."

"I am not your tool, Storm. I will not be lured by promises of your power."

"I'm not offering you *my* power," Storm murmured. "I'm offering you *yours*. I can teach you, in a single candlemark, what those who came before you needed a dozen turnings to learn. I can make you all that you should have been, an Adept of the Merik Orders, a sworn guardian of the innocent."

He chuckled with amusement.

"Of course, those sworn guardians betrayed their people to the Spehari and were, eventually, betrayed in turn. But in me, Teer of the Merik, the knowledge of the Orders survives. And I can give it to you."

Teer wasn't certain how exactly Storm was intending to "give" him knowledge—but the talk of a single candlemark suggested it wasn't going to involve him training with the callipsus as he'd trained with Tyrus.

The image of the massive man-eating lizard giving a classroom lecture—or even Tyrus's teaching style of standing at the student's shoulder and saying things like "Slow is learning, learning is skill, skill is speed"—brought an involuntary chuckle to Teer's dreaming mind.

Instead of answering, he focused his will on the dream and conjured the Kott-steel saber Kard had given him. Holding it out in front of him, he pointed it at Storm.

"Even if I was prepared to betray Taran, Kard is not, and I will not betray Kard," he told the monster. "There is no secret path through the defenses, and I wouldn't tell you about it if there were.

"This town has been fortified against you, and we know to look for your spawning ground now."

Storm sighed and shook his head.

"One life, child," he said calmly. "One life against hundreds. I offer you a chance to avoid the bloodshed and end the violence. Bring me

Taran, Teer of the Merik. Tell her what lies you wish, tell her what stories will guide her, but bring her forth from the houses and trenches and deliver her to me.

"Without their Captain-Magistrate, the army will freeze. My children will be safe and I will have no need to storm the Unity's defenses and burn this town around them. In her sacrifice, I would even meet the desire that drew me to your master and spare you that betrayal.

"One life against hundreds," he repeated. "Even Taran might make that choice willingly. And I will give you the knowledge of your Adepthood and you will save more."

Teer was surprised to realize he was tempted. Storm made a compelling case, and he spoke so smoothly, so convincingly, it took effort—hard in a dream!—to remember that the other being in his dream was actually a twelve-foot-tall carnivore that saw Teer's people as prey.

"This is only a dream," he said aloud. "I don't know how or why you have broken into my dreams, but you will find nothing for you here. Begone, monster. Dawn will see the truth in your lies."

"Dawn is a threshold," Storm replied. Teer wasn't even sure what the creature *meant*, but he suspected he wasn't agreeing. "Dawn is a beginning, but dawn is also an ending.

"We could make a deal, Teer of the Merik, to spare these poor fools their fate. But if you choose the slaughter to come, dawn will mark an ending. What comes is on your hands, my young friend."

"Blood is on the hands that shed it," Teer said stonily. "I'll not betray anyone. Not for a vague promise of knowledge torn from the minds of dead Merik. Get out of my head."

"I never entered your head. I merely opened a door and you came out to greet me," Storm said with a broad grin. "And while your choice could spare hundreds, all I truly need from you is for you to sleep.

"And you came to me of your own will."

The wind suddenly sharpened, a new edge of chilly frost adding to the air whipping past Teer as it accelerated. He barely had time to realize he'd made a massive mistake before he found himself in the center of a cyclone of ice and snow, an ever-swirling barrier trapping him in the prairie of lost dreams.

"You shield your will better without training than many I have seen with it," Storm told him, the callipsus's voice carrying through the cyclonic trap holding Teer's mind. "Even here, I do not believe I can *harm* you.

"But I can make certain that you do not leave. Rest well, Teer of the Merik. I do not intend that you will ever awaken."

20

Teer was not the type of introspective youth who thought much about his dreams or tried to control them. Summoning a mirage of Kard's power to drive Storm from his dream before had been one thing, but this was something else entirely.

He couldn't wake himself up. He wasn't even sure how to *try*, but just willing himself to wake did nothing. The wind cut at his skin, and he could feel frost forming and melting across his shoulders.

The wall of wind surrounded him in every direction. He couldn't even see the dream prairie that he'd foolishly walked onto to speak with Storm.

Swallowing and focusing his will, Teer tried to stride into the winds and push through. Blades of ice and sleet sliced into his skin, but he struggled to keep moving—right up until the wind strengthened and hurled him bodily back into the center of the cyclone.

Teer was surprised to realize he wasn't bleeding. Despite the power that was containing him, he appeared to be immune to *injury*—enough of him knew that this wasn't real to protect him from harm even inside the dream.

A distant thunder echoed through the dream, strange enough and powerful enough that he *knew* it was from the real world. He had no way to judge its true volume, but it didn't feel right to be the guns.

It was bigger. Uglier. Something very *wrong* was taking place in Shellsvan, but Teer was trapped in a dream hell he couldn't escape.

Another charge into the walls of wind achieved nothing more. The cold was starting to hurt, but he knew he was unharmed. Just trapped. The cold was part of the barrier, part of what held him, but it wasn't like he could create warmth.

Or could he? In this strange dreamspace, he'd summoned a mirror of Kard's power before to attack. But Teer had seen Kard summon power to light a campfire before, too.

He didn't have any wood, but if he could summon fire, that should warm the dreamscape. Maybe even enough that he could *think*—and the numbness in his hands and face was starting to get in the way of that.

He focused on his memory of the orange sparks he'd seen Kard use to call on fire magic, and on the image and sensation of fire. A fountain of orange light surged out from his hand, falling onto the ground and starting to pile up.

For a few heartbeats, that was all that happened. A small heap of glittering orange specks formed on the ground of the dream—and then, as if it crossed some invisible minimum, it burst into flame.

Heat rippled out from the fire with enough ferocity that Teer stepped backward. He tripped over the sword he'd conjured earlier and fell painfully into the storm walls.

The fire vanished as the storm flung him back into the center of the trap and almost into his conjured flame. The chill returned and Teer inhaled a long, ragged breath. Even in dreams, he lacked Kard's training and power. He could duplicate some of it, but he lacked the *understanding* to do anything with it.

Pulling himself back to his feet, he glared at the sword he'd tripped over.

He could conjure the fire again, but he wasn't sure it had helped other than to stave off some of the numbness. If he was careful, though, he could at least avoid his sword.

The sword.

Why was the sword still *there*? Like the fire, it was a thing he'd conjured into the dream and it should have vanished. Instead, it lay there on the ground, as solid as if he was looking at in the real world.

More. Once he was aware he was dreaming, he'd found the dream-scape Storm used to communicate with him had a vague sense of unreality to it. Even the trap holding him in place had that feeling. He was trapped in an illusion, one that he didn't have the will to overcome.

Except the Kott-steel blade lying on the ground felt more solid and real than anything else in the place. It had not vanished when he'd stopped paying attention to it. *Storm* had ignored it, clearly treating it as just another conjuring of dreamstuff, but Teer was wondering if it was that simple.

If a prince had to choose between his people and the gods, he carried a blade that could cut the gods.

There was something *more* to the blade forged by the strange people of the northern swamp. Something that had carried over into the dream when Teer had called the blade to him. The sword survived his lack of attention because the sword in some strange way was dreaming *its own* presence.

He picked it up, studying the dream of the sword. Shifting burgundy lines in the black steel caught the distorted light of the dream, glowing in the gray of the prairie storm the callipsus had trapped him with.

"Storm is not a god," he said aloud. "So, if you can cut gods…this should be nothing."

Teer had barely begun his training with the sword. He held it carefully, took a tentative swing to check that the balance in the dream was the same as the balance in reality—and he felt a strange warmth to the hilt that the weapon didn't have in waking life.

An eagerness that the blade couldn't communicate in daylight but that surged through Teer in the dream.

The sword dreamed its own presence there in the dream—and the sword knew both what he wanted of it and that *it could do it.*

"Okay. Let's dream it and see what happens," Teer told the blade.

He struck.

The saber was a slashing weapon. Tyrus had taught him enough to keep his strikes contained, an elbow-based blow instead of full shoulder-blow. The strike would have opened a man up from shoulder to groin, but he wasn't sure what he was expecting against the storm.

He wasn't expecting the storm to part like it was made of cloth. Rippling edges spun away from the cut for a few moments, then started to close back up—but Teer couldn't let that happen.

He struck again. And again. And again, until he'd cut open a path through the winds wide enough for him to walk through.

The moment he passed through the storm, the entire cyclone vanished. Hanging on to the hilt of the sword, he exhaled a long breath.

"Time to wake up," he told himself, focusing on the grip. This had to work. Storm's prison was broken. This had to—

Work.

Teer started awake. The Kott-steel sword was in his hand—he was *sure* he'd gone to bed with it in the harness next to the bed with the rest of his weapons, but there it was. He clamped down on the hilt with a furious strength and exhaled a deep sigh.

Then thunder rumbled through the air. It was still dark outside, but one of the cannons on Shellsvan's main street had just fired.

Except that the guns had been in pairs and only *one* gun fired. And Kard should have been in the room, but Teer was alone.

Gunfire crackled through the town. Even inside, Teer could tell it was still dark. Whatever nighttime defenses the Unity had put in place, they had clearly failed. Either the callipsuses were already in the town, or their illusions were.

He grabbed his gear, checking his ammunition pouches as he slung the two long guns over his back. The clearest sign that Kard had tried to wake him up was that his repeater cartridge pouch was open. His master had taken the handful of Tyrus's blessed bullets he had left— which, if he hadn't been able to wake Teer and recognized the problem, made perfect sense.

There were eight in Teer's repeater. That would have to be enough.

Teer could hear burning in the distance, but it sounded like the hotel Taran had used as a command post was empty except for him.

How long had he been sleeping?

Belting his armored jacket closed, he shook away the last dregs of the dream and the trap and focused on his link to Kard. The El-Spehari was still nearby, somewhere between the hotel and the jail over the wardstone.

Storm had taken Teer out of the beginning of the fight, but the Merik Hunter was awake now.

It was time to get to work.

———

As Teer stepped out into the flames and the chaos of Shellsvan, the pieces of the puzzle fell into place for him. First, he'd already seen that the callipsuses could handle explosives—like the blast-cotton they'd used to rig up the gully. Secondly, he'd heard from Avitus that the regiment's supply chain was a mess, which meant the Unity troops would have stockpiled as much in terms of ammunition for the artillery as possible.

And third, while the callipsuses tended to use their illusory abilities to lure their enemies into missteps and attacks on allies, that same magic could allow the big lizards to slip into the town and the Twenty-Fifth Horse Artillery's ammunition dump.

The explosion that had pierced his dreams had *leveled* the west end of town and taken out the guns positioned there. Debris had set many of the other buildings on fire, and it was clear that the Unity troops hadn't had a chance to try to fight the flames.

A dead callipsus was sprawled against the wall opposite the hotel, another victim of Tyrus's blessed bullets, Teer judged. The monsters were *in* the town, and Teer doubted anyone except Kard or Taran could fight the creatures.

As if to prove him wrong, the one remaining field gun in the center street roared again, a spray of fire and fist-sized stormshot blazing down the open area between the buildings.

Teer didn't know what the artillery team was shooting at, but watching the gout of fire and lead, his opinion of the team's ability to hurt a callipsus increased dramatically!

He charged out into the street, looking for the gun team's target and for the gun team itself—and as he moved, he felt power ripple through the city. A wave of green wardlight flickered out from the jail cell, washing over the town and then solidifying into place on the outskirts.

As the wardlight passed over them, the fires muted and the wind calmed. Whatever illusions the callipsuses were still calling faltered as Taran finally released the energies of the wardstone.

Teer hoped that the plan had worked. *He* needed to find Kard—but as he turned to warn the gun team not to shoot *him*, it became clear that while they had killed *one* callipsus at some point, their last shot hadn't done them any good.

The mound of battered and burned monster between him and the field gun was an impressive sign of the power of Unity artillery—except that as he located the five-soldier gun team, he saw the callipsus leap down from the roof of the burning building next to them, its ugly sickle claws slicing the cannon itself into pieces.

The soldiers didn't even have time to react. Claws and teeth flashed with brutal speed, and the last of the Unity guns was silenced. The monstrous lizard turned toward Teer, and he barely remembered drawing his repeater from the shoulder scabbard.

He fired as the callipsus tried to dodge. His first shot struck true, but illusions twisted around the monster and threw off his aim. His enemy couldn't *hide* from him with its magic, but they could confuse his eyes and break his normal near-perfect aim.

Two shots went wide, but the shot that *did* hit broke the callipsus's leg. It lost balance, causing him to miss with his fourth shot—and then managed to *leap* on its uninjured leg, crossing half the distance between them in a single bound.

Fear accelerated even *his* reflexes, and the last four shots in the repeater blazed out in a single stream of flame. Only one missed, and the callipsus staggered to a halt a handful of feet in front of Teer before it collapsed onto the ground.

"Storms and Pillars," he swore. Shellsvan awake was more of a nightmare than the *actual* nightmare Storm had trapped him in. He needed to get to Kard.

Because unless his boss and partner had changed dramatically overnight, Kard was with Taran, guarding the wardstone—and *the scent of air after the storm* would go straight for the stone.

Teer could—*would*—hate the elder callipsus for everything he had done, but in a twisted way, he was beginning to understand the monster. Storm would recognize the trap and would act to break it to free whatever portion of his clan was trapped.

Shellsvan was already ruined. The only question was whether Taran's gambit would pay off and destroy the callipsus clan.

2 2

———————

The link between Teer and Kard served as his compass. The town wasn't large enough for him to get lost in at the worst of times, but knowing exactly which way he needed to go was still helpful—though he'd have headed toward the stone-built jail regardless.

With the ward raised and the callipsuses' illusions muted, the gunfire had quieted. Part of that, Teer grimly suspected, was that most of the soldiers in the town itself were already dead. Any callipsuses outside the ward had likely fallen back, waiting to see the fate of their kin inside the barrier.

The ones inside were almost certainly gathering to their father. The last smatter of gunfire fell to silence as he reached the jail building— and a strange hush blanketed the town in its absence.

The wooden buildings were still burning, but the fires were muted by the power of the ward—and the sound of the remaining fire was muffled even further. The hush was unnatural, and Teer could guess where it was coming from.

Storm was coming.

The jail had been reinforced since the previous evening, with the door he'd entered through last blocked entirely by sandbags and the windows barricaded from the inside with wood, metal plates and even more sandbags.

Circling the building, Teer found the entrance at the same time as he found a pair of dead callipsuses. At least, he *guessed* it had been two. The bodies had been violently blown apart by powerful magic, and he could almost *taste* the leftover power of the spell that had killed them.

"Don't shoot," he called out, approaching the door with his hands spread wide. "It's Teer."

"Thank the Courts, get in here!" Kard bellowed—as able to sense Teer as Teer was able to sense him in turn.

A barricade of the same metal, wood and sandbags that blocked the windows half-filled the rear entrance to the jail. It took some effort and help from Kard for Teer to get over it—and he found himself face-to-face with the last of the ten-pounder field guns.

At this distance, he could see that it resembled nothing so much as a scaled-up version of his stepfather's hunter. A long-barreled breechloader built of blued steel, its muzzle looked almost big enough for Teer to put his head into.

Part of that, he suspected, was that it was pointed right at his face.

"Taran got the two outside," Kard told him. "The gun is our first line of defense, though I'm not sure we'll get a chance to reload it. You can feel it, can't you?"

"Storm is smothering sound in the town to conceal their approach," Teer guessed. "Where's Taran?"

"In the basement, trying not to pass out," the El-Spehari said. "Boosting a wardstone from nothing takes a lot of energy—and unlike maintaining it, you can't do it with an execution."

Teer shivered. He hadn't *forgotten*, really, that wardstones were often charged by hanging people over them. The threat had been used on him at one point, after all.

It just hadn't occurred to him that killing someone might be the easiest way to wake up Shellsvan's wardstone. It was probably a good thing that wasn't an option—he wasn't sure if his opinion of Taran would have survived discovering whether she'd murder someone in cold blood for her plan!

"You've a plan?" Teer asked, glancing around the hall. The back entrance led into a cramped corridor barely big enough for the gun they were now standing behind. A gray-uniformed gunner crouched next to the weapon, ready to fire it once a callipsus breached the barricade, and a handful of cavalry troopers were in position to form a rough firing line.

Not that their guns would do much against callipsuses. The cannon would have some effect, but Teer was grimly aware he was out of Tyrus's bullets.

"Hold," Kard said quietly. "I don't know if there's anyone else left alive inside the ward, but they've got to breach the cellar if they want to escape. So, they have to come to us, and we've blocked every way in except this one."

The El-Spehari paused for a long breath.

"Do you have any blessed bullets left?" he finally asked.

"No. You?"

"No," Kard admitted. "Dragonshot can kill the big bastards—I wasn't actually sure of that, so thank the moons for small mercies. But without those bullets…"

Without those bullets, their best ways to hurt the callipsuses were the Kott-steel sabers—and Kard's magic.

Magic that Kard couldn't use around the Unity troops. A single report to Taran could turn their most powerful ally against them—and Teer, at least, had no idea how powerful the compulsion of the Midnight Proclamation would be.

"How many rounds do you have?" Teer asked the gunner.

"Twelve," the woman said grimly. "All canister. Three dragonshot, three stormshot, six regular. Anything else…"

She shrugged.

"Was either with the other guns or in the ammo dump," Kard concluded. "The monsters knew where to hit to weaken us. Dragonshot and stormshot *should* kill them. And there shouldn't be more than six of them left inside the ward…"

Shouldn't was carrying a lot of weight in that sentence. They'd already killed more callipsuses than anyone had expected to face when Teer and Kard had come west to hunt Storm. Taran's entire *army* had been intended to fight *one*.

Teer loosened the saber in its scabbard, wishing for some sense of the warm certainty the blade had carried in his dream.

"We will be ready," he said quietly. "My sword can cut their hide—and when all else fails, Taran should be able to help soon, yes?"

"Right," Kard replied, with a certainty that Teer *knew* he didn't feel. Reading his master's emotions made helpful lies even more useless. "We—"

A strangely muffled explosion interrupted the gunner's words, and Teer felt the ground shiver beneath his feet.

"That was close," the gunner snapped. "It *felt* close. Didn't…sound close."

"They're muffling sound. But why would there be—"

"The cellar is in loose soil," Teer interrupted Kard. "They're not bothering with *us*. They're going straight to the wardstone!"

He felt Kard's understanding, but he was already moving.

"Hold the door," he heard Kard order before the older Hunter took off after him.

Teer had his sword drawn by the time he reached the door to the cellar. The heavy door was a lesser barrier than the one beneath it, he knew, and even so, he hesitated as he considered it.

Kard did not. Magic blasted past Teer and tore the door from its hinges—and his boss charged past him, wearing his true face.

The Midnight Proclamation was a problem for after the dawn, Teer supposed. For now, they needed to *survive*.

SOME TINY PORTION of the universe still appeared to be on their side. The hole that Storm had blasted into the cellar had opened on the wrong side of the vault door. That appeared to have bought them some time.

Not enough time. The terrifying sharpness of the callipsuses' hind claws had sheared through metal and wood with ease—and while Teer had usually seen the beings standing to their full height, it appeared they were perfectly *capable* of moving with their torsos horizontal.

The low ceilings hadn't slowed the callipsuses down. The vault door *had*, but now it was gone. The space barely felt large enough for *one* of the massive creatures, but Teer saw *four* of them snarling and pushing in on the defensive shield Taran was maintaining around the ward.

She wasn't fighting back. Just holding a bubble of force around the wardstone, herself...and Kye, who lay crumpled against the stone where a blow had clearly thrown her.

Teer's sword was in his hand, and he turned his charge down the stairs into a lunge he hoped Tyrus would have been proud of. The closest callipsus was still turning in response to Kard's blasting the door apart when Teer's blade tore into its tail and leg.

A scream echoed in the enclosed space as Teer ripped his sword out of the monster's flesh and brought it around in a horizontal chop that cleaved through the callipsus's spine and torso in a single strike.

Kard's magic blasted past him, only to be grounded by a sudden intensification of the muffling effect.

A familiar scent somehow hit Teer's nostrils, overwhelming the smell of fire and blood and death in the vault, and he realized that Storm had clearly found less-direct uses of his powers. Muffled, Kard's magic failed to injure the callipsus he was aiming for—and Teer couldn't even *see* Storm.

All three of the still-living callipsuses he could see had both eyes.

Then Storm was there. Somehow smaller than he had been in the yard of the farmhouse a handful of days before, like he'd shunted some of his size *elsewhere* to allow him to maneuver in the confined space.

Teer parried a slash from the monster's massive dewclaw—and Storm struck while he was ever so slightly off-balance. The callipsus's hand hit him in the face, stunning him and jerking his head back.

A thick taste of alien blood filled his mouth as his sword slipped from suddenly nerveless fingers. Teer tried to work his cheeks and tongue to spit out whatever the monster had put through his lips, but a spike of power overwhelmed his senses.

The blood was suddenly warm—and then his mind was suddenly full of new images, thoughts, stories…memories.

Overwhelmed as an entire other life crashed into his brain, Teer fell.

23

*A*bray was on the ground. Abray wasn't sure how he'd ended up on the ground. Or where he was. Everything was weird and muddled.

Abray wasn't Abray. *That* was why he didn't know why he was on the ground.

Abray's last memory was of a large set of jaws closing over his face after a battle he'd almost won. *Teer's* last memory was of Storm shoving blood into his mouth and then pulsing power through it.

Abray/Teer saw the wicked claw descend from above. Both lives gave the same instinctive response and they dodged sideways. The callipsus made a disgruntled noise—but it wasn't like the creature could speak.

Both Abray's and Teer's memories included dream conversations with *the scent of air after the storm.* In Abray's memories, the creature's dream avatar had both eyes. In Teer's, he didn't.

Abray's instincts gave commands that Teer's muscles didn't know how to execute. Magic and panic alike flared through his body, and he spasmed sideways in a manner he hadn't thought was physically *possible.*

It wasn't enough this time, and Storm's dewclaw sliced through muscle and flesh as it scored along the bone of his arm.

Memories flared in response to the pain—a different battle. Memories of a log cabin steeped in grief, and of a hunt unlike anything *Teer* had ever done.

An ambush. *Storm* ambushed, not ambushing, as Abray put an arrow into the monster's eye. The mistake had been thinking that the yard-long shaft with its barbed head had been enough to cripple Storm, even if the callipsus had survived. The thunderbuss had been torn from Abray's hands as he'd moved in to finish the job.

Storm had lost an eye, but with his bow left behind and his gun wrecked, even an Adept of the Merik Orders couldn't defeat a callipsus in hand-to-hand combat. His big hunting knife had left its mark on the callipsus—Teer could see the scars where Abray remembered piercing the monster's hide through sheer magical strength—but Abray had *died*.

And Teer now *remembered* dying. Remembered pain. Remembered the physical pain being nothing to the emotional pain and grief.

Another man's grief empowered his limbs, and Teer was suddenly on his feet, dodging past a driving claw with the speed of training Teer didn't have.

He'd lost precious heartbeats. Kard was wounded—he didn't remember that. The three younger callipsuses were pressing on the shield.

Memories of betrayal surged through Teer. A burning monastery. Spehari and El-Spehari swearing oaths—and then the same Spehari laughing while the abbey burned.

Running. Hunting. Fighting the same monster in front of him now.

Teer dodged again. He was bleeding. There was nothing he could do about that. Kard was slumped against the wall, dark magic spinning around his head and overwhelming him.

It was on Teer. Storm's magic now surged at the youth, and his vision blacked out.

But memory remained. Blindfolds worn in the monastery training yard. An instructor's voice.

"Your senses are your greatest power," a long-dead woman said in

Teer's head. "Without them, all of your strength, all of your magic, is meaningless. With them, you can overcome *anything*."

The sound. The touch of moving air, driven by Storm's claws. Memory of where the sword had fallen—and if *Teer* didn't know how to use a sword all that well, *Abray* did.

Teer dove. Guided by sound and wind, he slid under Storm's outstretched claws and reached the Kott-steel blade.

Abray's memories spoke of skills and patterns. Teer's muscles didn't know those patterns, but he could follow the memory. He could follow the *pattern*.

To his feet. Guard upper right. The sound and feeling of *impact*— and his sight returned as will and Kott steel alike drove back the callipsus's power. A freshly detached claw clattered on the roughly paved floor.

Storm had made a mistake. Whatever he'd done with blood and memory had disabled Teer, but he hadn't *finished* Teer—and buried in the memories were the skills Teer needed to fight him.

Guard lower right. Blade on claw, but callipsus claws were steel-hard. It was more like parrying a sword than cutting through a claw.

Guard lower right *again*. This time, Teer was faster than Storm, and another claw went flying.

Guard upper left, a transition through the air in front of Teer that caught a full leg-kick and parried the massive dewclaw. The clash of metal on metal sounded *wrong* for that impact, but it sent Storm reeling backward.

Then Storm's power *pulsed* again. Not triggering illusions. Triggering *memories*.

A redheaded Rolin woman in the forest. Injured. Wolfen had ambushed her party. Their venom was in her veins; she would die soon. Abray should have just walked away. He should have given her mercy, if he had to do *something*.

But Abray had sworn oaths. Those oaths had been used to manipulate his Order and, in the end, as a reason to burn them to the ground —but he'd sworn them nonetheless.

He'd cursed himself for a fool, but he'd assembled a sled from the wreckage of the woman's wagon and hauled her back to his cabin. A combination of hard-won new herbal knowledge and the magic of an Adept allowed him to heal her over time.

She'd lost her husband to the wolfen, monsters with venomous teeth and claws. Abray had saved her life, but he wanted nothing to do with people anymore. People would only bring the Spehari to him.

Still, Opal had insisted he visit her in the village she eventually ended up in. And, when she could, she visited him.

One day she just…never left. And it was comfortable. She hunted. He hunted. She went into the village and bought things from the Unity. He couldn't. He *was* hunted, marked for death by the Unity.

And then one day, he came back from hunting to find that she was dead, her skull torn open.

Abray's grief tore through Teer as Storm played on the dead man's memories like a fiddle. The distraction let the callipsus strike this time, and his dewclaw sank deep into Teer's belly.

Where Teer, driven by Abray's rage, *grabbed it*. Unbalanced, standing on one leg with the other *stuck* in Teer's flesh, the callipsus wavered…and fell.

The saber was still in Teer's hand. He wasn't sure how—surely, he'd dropped it as Abray's memories shattered him?—but there it was.

He struck.

Muscle and bone parted far too easily beneath the keen edge of the Kott-steel sword. The monster's leg was still attached to Teer…but it was no longer attached to *Storm*.

Still holding the dewclaw into his stomach to stanch the bleeding, Teer let Abray's memories guide the sword. Half-turn. Blade high.

Executioner's strike.

Storm's head rolled free before Teer even fully realized what he'd done.

HOLDING the monster's claw inside his abdomen wasn't the best plan to keep himself from bleeding out, Teer knew; it was just the only one he could think of. Blood loss from his wounded arm was rippling through him as well as the continued cascade of new memories.

He was only *Teer* in his own head about half the time. Abray had lived for over sixty turnings. Born in a similar fishing village to Teer, he'd spent his teenage seasons working to become an Adept—and then half a dozen turnings after that learning to *be* an Adept.

Time was strange. Abray hadn't paid much attention to calendars, and neither had Teer. Neither of them had any real idea when the monastery had burned.

Abray had hated Spehari and El-Spehari, though, and he knew nothing of the Sunset Rebellion. Even Teer's bond to Kard was a frail barrier against the scale of the Unity's betrayal of the Merik Orders.

Abray hadn't been senior enough to truly understand what had happened, and there were no records or stories of it that Teer was aware of. Abray only knew that Unity troops led by El-Spehari commanders had stormed his monastery and burned it to the ground.

He might not have been the only one to escape, but he didn't *know* of any others.

And now all of his memories were in Teer's head. Three times as many turnings of memories as Teer had of his own. Abray had kept his skills up in exile, but his training had been thirty-plus turnings past when he'd died and Storm had eaten his memories.

The memories churned without Teer's conscious will. Abray knew that he'd known something, which collided with Teer's thoughts as the memories of a dead man tried to guide the mind of the living one to the key point.

Self-healing. A meditative trance—one that required safety but allowed awareness, channeling energy to heal wounds that would otherwise be fatal.

The lesson snapped into Teer's head in full clarity—along with the realization that Storm's death had released Kard from whatever had bound him. The callipsuses were now trapped between *two* magical shields—one protecting Kye and one protecting Teer.

Containing the callipsuses appeared to be entirely secondary for the shields, as the two demigods shielded their charges and unleashed their power on their enemies.

Still, that protection allowed Abray to pull on his memories and bring Teer into the right positions to open the energy flow. Taking a deep breath, they removed the claw from their abdomen and *focused*.

It was funny. The focus of Teer's power and energy was now inside himself, burning away infection and dirt and knitting flesh and skin back together. Yet he was strangely aware of the battle around him.

The Unity would never have sent two El-Spehari against three callipsuses—let alone the *thirty* or so that they'd ended up fighting—but if they'd had to pick two, Taran and Kard should have been the ones they'd sent.

Taran was an expert at fighting this foe. Even through the trance, Teer could tell that. Every motion, every spell, was carefully balanced against the strengths and weaknesses of the callipsuses. She was young, but she was powerful and she *knew* this enemy.

Kard, though… Kard didn't know the enemy as well, but he made up for it with experience and power. What Taran achieved by knowing her foes, *he* achieved by knowing *himself*.

In that underground cellar, Teer truly saw Lord Colonel Karn of House Morais for the first time, the warrior-mage who had served at the right hand of the Prince in Sunset.

Trapped between the two El-Spehari, the callipsuses were doomed. They didn't have Storm's ability to mute Spehari magic or blind the Mages with their own powers. They had illusions and muscles and terrifyingly sharp claws—and it was not enough.

They fell and silence followed them. The magical shields collapsed, and Teer/Abray could sense/see the two El-Spehari facing each other across the corpses of their enemy.

The muffling over the town was fading, he realized—and dawn was rising with it. Natural light filtered through the hole the callipsuses had blasted into the basement.

Teer was going to live. He knew that now. Abray's memories had guided him to a form of healing that would preserve him. It wasn't as fast as Kard's healing magic, and it might not be as non-scarring as Kotan poultices, but he would survive what should have been a fatal wound.

Assuming that the dim light of dawn wasn't about to show him Kard's death, that was.

24

"Karn."

The name hung in the dawn light like a ticking bomb.

"I tried so hard not to suspect, but there is a limit."

"I know. But the alternative was failure and death, so here we are," Kard told his old apprentice.

The anger running through Teer's new memories said to just let the two El-Spehari kill each other. He'd bought enough goodwill to get out alive.

"The irony is not lost on me. I am alive because of you," Taran conceded. "But we both know that, thanks to your little rebellion, not all of my choices are my own."

"We did not create the Midnight Proclamation," Kard said.

"No. But what choice did you leave our King? Bind us or destroy us."

"How about *trust* you? You and three score others never betrayed him. Never wavered in your loyalty, not even when the Sunset Banners flew outside the City of the Pillars itself!"

Teer watched Kard shake his head sadly and wondered what

memories were running through his partner's mind. *He* had never been to the City of the Pillars.

Abray apparently had. It was a memory touched with a mixture of disdain and awe. When he'd been there, it had been as part of a group of Adepts sworn to the service of the King in Winter. The city was immense and carefully designed, even Abray's *memories* of it stunning to Teer—but all Abray's memories of the Unity were marked with his rage and disgust at their betrayal.

"It doesn't matter now, does it? I swore to the Midnight Proclamation, submitted my will to that of my King. And now I know who and what you are, my old teacher. Wounded and battered as we both are, I still have no choice.

"Yield. I can heal your friend and Kye alike, but you must surrender and submit to the King and his Proclamation. If you do not, I must destroy you."

"I can heal them both as well," Kard offered. "All you have to do is let us walk away, Taran. I am not your enemy. I'm not even the King in Winter's enemy anymore. I just refuse to be a slave."

Not many in the Unity had that privilege, in Teer's experience. The difference in rights and authority between a Spehari and even a Unity army officer was horrifying. There were rules and laws for how the Unity's people could act—and *none* of them applied to a Spehari.

Teer had nearly been executed for trying to kill Kard—but if a Spehari had decided to kill Teer in the street, that would have been perfectly fine. The Unity's laws were for its subjects, not its rulers.

"Your actions left *me* no choice on that count," Taran told him. She half-turned away from Kard, kneeling and channeling power into Kye. Teer's awareness through the trance wasn't enough to tell how injured the officer was or even how tired Taran was.

He knew the situation was a mess. Taran could argue and try to convince Kard, but she *couldn't* let him go any more than Teer could raise his hand against Kard. Her bond to the Midnight Proclamation and the King in Winter left her no choice.

And Teer couldn't do anything yet. He could tell that breaking the healing trance would be a bad, *bad* idea. He needed more time and he had no idea how to tell Kard that.

"I won't hurt you," Kard said quietly. "But I will not submit to the King in Winter. Take your victory, Taran, and let us go."

"Why do you even bother, Karn? You know the strength of the magic that binds me. You know the power of our King. The Midnight Proclamation is clear: all El-Spehari must submit to His Will or be destroyed."

She still had her back turned to Kard. Even *Teer* could tell she was making herself vulnerable—but he suspected it was more of a trap than an invitation.

"I will not fight you," Kard repeated.

"Then submit."

"No."

Taran nodded, helping Kye up onto the wardstone and finally turning back to Kard. She carried no weapons, not even any of the redcrystal artifacts of her arcane art. She was far from unarmed, though, and Teer didn't know enough to judge whether she or Kard was the stronger mage.

Abray's memories said that raising the ward should have worn her down enough that Kard could take her—though Teer's link to Kard told him the El-Spehari was badly weakened by his own wounds and whatever spell Storm had used to take him out of the fight.

Kye wasn't going to have any impact in this. Taran had spent enough energy to make sure her lover was going to be fine, but Teer knew *exactly* how effective shooting at Kard with regular guns was.

It was down to the two El-Spehari, neither of whom wanted to start the fight.

"You don't have the option to not fight and not yield, my old teacher," Taran said. She picked up a rope, probably used to help guide the wardstone into the basement, and tossed it to Kard.

"You expect me to tie myself up, do you?" Kard asked drily. "Just because I don't want to fight you doesn't mean I'm going to hand you the prize my father has hunted for fifteen turnings."

He tossed the rope aside, leaving it to uncoil across the floor and reach Teer's feet.

"Those are your choices, Karn," Taran told him. "Yield or fight me. I cannot let you leave."

Teer could *feel* the power sparking between the two El-Spehari as they faced each other. Magical and emotional tension filled the cellar as they stood.

There was no anger in the room; that was the strangest part to him. Fear, sadness, grief, bitterness... He could feel all of those things rippling off Kard especially and *see* them in Taran's pose, but neither of them was angry.

The angriest person in the room was *him*, Abray's memories of Spehari and El-Spehari betrayal warring with memories of Storm's murder of his wife and Teer's own memories of Kard sparing his life.

With a final *push* of energy, he released both a long breath and the healing trance.

Keeping his motions small, he hooked the rope over to him with his toes. Whatever else Teer might have become, he had *been* a ranch hand. A cowboy.

He knew what to do with a rope. The standoff between the two Mages was only going to end in violence, and the best way *he* could see to end it was, well, for one of the Mages to end up bound.

And he wasn't planning on delivering *Kard* to the Pillars his friend feared.

"Well?" Taran asked.

Teer moved. This was not Abray's skill. This was *Teer's* skill—guided and aided by Abray's knowledge and the magic the two men shared. The rope snapped out, catching and wrapping around Taran's legs in a motion that would have made his old cattlehand teachers proud.

He twisted the rope, knotting it around the El-Spehari and pulling toward him. Between Adept speed and Adept strength, he wasn't sure Taran *could* have reacted in time to stop him before she fell.

Teer didn't have a *next* step, but Abray's memories cynically told him that Kard would. Power flared in the cellar again, blue sparks of mind magic flickering between the two El-Spehari as Taran hit the ground.

She fell limply, like her strings had been cut—but even as Kye started to go for her gun, a loud, tearing snore echoed through the cellar.

"Leave your gun, little one," Kard told the Zeeanan officer. "She's fine. She's just asleep."

Kye slumped backward, exhaustion warring with anger as she glared at Teer and Kard.

"You will pay for that," she whispered.

"More than you can possibly imagine," Kard agreed. "Teer, are you all right?"

"No," Teer/Abray whispered. "We need to go."

"On that, we are agreed. But I have to heal her."

"Leave her," Abray demanded.

Kard looked at him oddly, likely recognizing that the demand was out of character for Teer.

"I will not," the El-Spehari replied. "I *cannot*. She was my student and is my friend, regardless of what is between us now. And she is injured."

He knelt over Taran for a few moments, his power visibly flowing into her wounds to Teer's eyes. For his part, Teer watched Kye to make sure she left her quickshooter in her holster.

"She'll sleep for about a candlemark," Kard finally told Kye. "If you can get help to get her to a proper bed, that will help her finish healing. *You* need to rest as well."

"Thank you," she said bitterly. "This…this…"

"This was a nightmare and a victory alike," the El-Spehari told her. "And I have doomed myself."

He shrugged.

"It is a price I knowingly paid," he concluded, echoing what Storm had told Teer earlier in the dreamscape. "Keep her safe, Lieutenant Kye." Kard chuckled. "And if you could refrain from telling the cavalry they have any reason to chase me for, oh, half a day…I'd appreciate it."

25

*S*hellsvan was basically gone.

The debris from the exploding ammunition dump had set large chunks of the town on fire—and what the ammo dump had missed, the guns using dragonshot canister against the callipsuses had lit up.

The ward still shimmered around the wreckage of the town. Teer and Kard passed through it without any difficulty—thanks to Abray's memories, Teer knew that Kard had opened a small portal for them.

The ward itself would remain at maximum strength until sunset or until Taran woke up and opened it. Given how little movement or life Teer had seen as they passed through the town, he doubted it would make much difference for the folks left behind.

There might well only be the single gunnery team and cavalry wing that had been dug into the jail *left*.

The trenches outside the ward were in better shape. There'd definitely been *some* trouble out there, with debris from the ammo-dump explosion having set sections on fire, but without the callipsuses actively in the fray, it looked like most of the cavalry troops *outside* the ward were fine.

Hundreds of Unity soldiers were dead, but the callipsuses were gone. Any survivors had fled.

And while *Teer* could mourn the cavalry troopers who'd helped and been friendly to them, Abray's memories still wrapped around every symbol, every gray uniform, and wove a layer of rage he couldn't quite control.

"Sir Hunter!"

Teer barely recognized Sergeant Tavis, the man in charge of the Seventy-Third's horse stables. Abray's memories were overwhelming his.

"Sergeant. Our horses?" Kard asked. "This situation appears resolved and we have business elsewhere."

"Are you… Are you sure, Sir Hunter?" Tavis asked. "We can't get into the ward. Did you get out?"

"The Captain-Magistrate let us out, yes," Kard replied. "The callipsuses inside are dead, but Teer and I need to hunt the spawning ground and destroy the eggs—or all of this might have been for nothing!"

That was an argument that definitely got through to Tavis, who led them to where Star and Clack were stabled.

"Your saddlebags are here too. Should I pull together some supplies for you?" Tavis asked.

Teer bit down an angry response. He was *not* Abray. He didn't need to yell at a helpful ally over a dead man's rage.

He didn't *think* he was Abray. It was hard. He had the memories of an entire life—two, in some ways, given that Abray had gone into exile and spent twenty turnings as a hermit and husband.

Half-unconsciously, he walked into the stall and rubbed Star's neck. The mare shoved her nose into his neck and whinnied. She was worried—she could tell something was wrong.

She was also solid. Like the sword in his dream, she was more solid than anything else, cutting through the haze of his mixed memories.

"Teer?" Kard asked softly. "What's going on?"

"Not here," Teer told him. Abray's memories said not to tell him at all, but Teer *needed* Kard to understand. "We need to be safe. On the road."

———

THEY RODE IN SILENCE, Teer struggling to balance out himself against Abray. One of the odder things he realized from the overwhelming presence of the dead man in his head was that he, Teer, had never loved.

He'd *cared*, and he'd *dallied*, and he'd had relationships, but he had never truly, deeply loved. Abray had. Abray's memories of Opal carried a level of passion and grief that he could lose himself in. It was when he considered those married seasons and Abray's revenge against Storm that he was at the greatest risk of losing himself to Abray.

But Star was there, the mare solid and steady and reminding him of who he was.

"Here," Kard finally declared, pulling them off the road toward a small brook flanked by trees. "I think there's a campsite and we should be safe from pursuit for now."

"What about the spawning ground?" Teer/Abray asked, the youth unsure if they could pursue it and the dead man assuming the El-Spehari had lied.

"I would *love* to hunt it down," Kard said. "But we can't. Taran will focus on it, most likely—use it as an excuse to give us some more time. She doesn't want to hunt me.

"But she has to." He shrugged as he dismounted, studying a small clearing in the trees. "This will do."

"So, what, we just leave it to her?" Teer asked sharply.

"If nothing else, I have almost as much faith in Taran as I do in you," Kard told him. "And that's before whatever is in your mind. Something's wrong, Teer. I can *feel* it. There's magic at play here."

"Callipsus magic," Teer agreed, struggling to focus on *his* memories, *his* friendship with Kard. Not Abray's anger. "Storm…Storm…put someone else's memories in my head. Someone he *ate* a long time ago."

"That is potentially one of the worst concepts I have ever considered," Kard said slowly. "Sit, Teer. Tell me, what you can, while I get camp set.

"You need to rest a bit."

Teer obeyed, slowly dismounting from Star and removing his saddlebags. He needed to groom her, but it could wait a bit. He left her to graze and collapsed onto a fallen log, watching Kard go through the efficient motions of setting up camp.

He figured that Kard needed the familiarity of that routine as much as Teer needed to rest.

"Storm kept offering me the knowledge of how to be an *Adept of the Merik Orders* as a payment for betraying first you and then Taran," Teer confessed. "I guess...he figured there was a chance I'd take the offer, and he had it ready?

"So, when he wanted to take me out of the fight, he dumped all of the memories of a man named Abray—who was an Adept of the Merik Orders—into me."

Kard exhaled a deep sigh.

"The scariest part to me," he said slowly, "out of the whole thing around your magic and the existence of these Adepts and Orders...is that *I* knew almost nothing about them. It has been fifteen turnings since the end of Sunset. Between the Prince in Sunset and the Unity, I served the Spehari and El-Spehari for *ninety* turnings.

"And in those hundred and five turnings, during many of which I was among the most trusted elites of the Unity, I barely heard of the Merik Orders. My father's people destroyed them *that* thoroughly."

Abray's anger spiked through Teer again, fraying his hold.

"Abray has a lot of memories of their betrayal," Teer said carefully. "And they're my memories now. I can't... I can only barely tell what's mine and what's his."

Kard had started the fire and was heating water, digging through his saddlebags for something specific.

"That is magic beyond anything I know," he admitted. "Memories, personalities, souls...I guess? These aren't things of Spehari magic. Or Kotan magic—or Merik magic, I suppose."

"I remember his training," Teer said. "I think...I think I can practice it. Learn it. Become an Adept and use my gifts."

"That's good," Kard allowed. "But you need to not lose yourself."

The El-Spehari smiled weakly but determinedly.

"It's been a nightmare of a day, but I think I know at least one way to help there."

Teer looked confused as Kard removed a package of some kind and dumped its contents into the hot water—and then the smell hit him.

When Teer had left his mother and stepfather's ranch, his mother had sent him away with dozens of packs of her dried stew mixes. Her meals had no right to be as good as they were when they were rehydrated, and these days, Teer figured there was literal magic to them.

At that moment, though, all that mattered was that they were *her* meals. Teer's mother's meals.

And through that smell, he could tell which memories were truly Teer.

For a while, at least.

JOIN THE MAILING LIST

Love Glynn Stewart's books? Join the mailing list at

Be the first to find out when new books are released!

ABOUT THE AUTHOR

Glynn Stewart is the author of *Starship's Mage*, a bestselling science fiction and fantasy series where faster-than-light travel is possible–but only because of magic. His other works include science fiction series *Duchy of Terra*, *Castle Federation* and *Vigilante*, as well as the urban fantasy series *ONSET* and *Changeling Blood*.

Writing managed to liberate Glynn from a bleak future as an accountant. With his personality and hope for a high-tech future intact, he lives in Southern Ontario with his partner, their cats, and an unstoppable writing habit.

VISIT GLYNNSTEWART.COM FOR NEW RELEASE UPDATES

CREDIT

The following people were involved in making this book:
Copyeditor: Richard Shealy
Proofreader: M Parker Editing
Cover art: Roman Chalyi
Typo Hunter Team
Faolan's Pen Publishing team: Jack, Kate, and Robin.

facebook.com/glynnstewartauthor

OTHER BOOKS BY GLYNN STEWART

For release announcements join the mailing list or visit **GlynnStewart.com**

STARSHIP'S MAGE

Starship's Mage
Hand of Mars
Voice of Mars
Alien Arcana
Judgment of Mars
UnArcana Stars
Sword of Mars
Mountain of Mars
The Service of Mars
A Darker Magic
Mage-Commander
Beyond the Eyes of Mars
Nemesis of Mars
Chimera's Star *(upcoming)*

Starship's Mage: Red Falcon
Interstellar Mage
Mage-Provocateur
Agents of Mars

Starship's Mage Novellas
Pulsar Race
Mage-Queen's Thief *(upcoming)*

DUCHY OF TERRA

The Terran Privateer
Duchess of Terra
Terra and Imperium
Darkness Beyond
Shield of Terra
Imperium Defiant
Relics of Eternity
Shadows of the Fall
Eyes of Tomorrow

SCATTERED STARS

Scattered Stars: Conviction

Conviction
Deception
Equilibrium
Fortitude
Huntress
Prodigal

Scattered Stars: Evasion

Evasion
Discretion
Absolution *(upcoming)*

PEACEKEEPERS OF SOL

Raven's Peace
The Peacekeeper Initiative
Raven's Course
Drifter's Folly
Remnant Faction
Raven's Flag *(upcoming)*

EXILE

Exile
Refuge
Crusade
Ashen Stars: An Exile Novella

CASTLE FEDERATION

Space Carrier Avalon
Stellar Fox
Battle Group Avalon
Q-Ship Chameleon
Rimward Stars
Operation Medusa
A Question of Faith: A Castle Federation Novella

Dakotan Confederacy

Admiral's Oath
To Stand Defiant
Unbroken Faith *(upcoming)*

AETHER SPHERES

Nine Sailed Star
Void Spheres *(upcoming)*

VIGILANTE
(WITH TERRY MIXON)

Heart of Vengeance
Oath of Vengeance

**Bound By Stars: A Vigilante Series
(With Terry Mixon)**
Bound By Law
Bound by Honor
Bound by Blood

TEER AND KARD

Wardtown
Blood Ward
Blood Adept

CHANGELING BLOOD

Changeling's Fealty
Hunter's Oath
Noble's Honor
Fae, Flames & Fedoras: A Changeling Blood Novella

ONSET

ONSET: To Serve and Protect
ONSET: My Enemy's Enemy
ONSET: Blood of the Innocent
ONSET: Stay of Execution
Murder by Magic: An ONSET Novella

STAND ALONE NOVELS & NOVELLAS

Children of Prophecy
City in the Sky
Excalibur Lost: A Space Opera Novella
Balefire: A Dark Fantasy Novella
Icebreaker: A Fantasy Naval Thriller

www.ingramcontent.com/pod-product-compliance
Lightning Source LLC
Chambersburg PA
CBHW031407310726
48971CB00003B/772